SOULS
Unchained

by

C.C. Wood

Cover by
Jena Brignola, Bibliophile Productions

Editing by
Tania Marinaro, Libros Evolution

Interior by
Paul Salvette, BB eBooks

Table of Contents

Chapter One 1

Chapter Two 11

Chapter Three 19

Chapter Four 25

Chapter Five 35

Chapter Six 45

Chapter Seven 57

Chapter Eight 67

Chapter Nine 73

Chapter Ten 79

Chapter Eleven 89

Chapter Twelve 99

Chapter Thirteen 111

Chapter Fourteen 117

Chapter Fifteen 127

Chapter Sixteen 137

Chapter Seventeen 147

Chapter Eighteen 159

Chapter Nineteen 169

Chapter Twenty 175

Chapter Twenty-One 185

Chapter Twenty-Two 195

Chapter Twenty-Three 201

Chapter Twenty-Four 205

Chapter Twenty-Five 213

Chapter Twenty-Six.. 219

Chapter Twenty-Seven 227

Chapter Twenty-Eight 235

Epilogue.. 243

Sign Up for C.C.'s Monthly Newsletter 249

About C.C. 250

Titles by C.C. Wood..................................... 251

To Michelle L.

Thank you for showing me around Austin and helping me figure out where Savannah and Rhys would probably live. It was the most fun I've ever had doing research!

Author's Note

Hi, Reader! First of all, thank you so much for picking up this copy of Souls Unchained. It means so much to me that you take the time to read my books, especially with so many other wonderful authors out there. When you're done, please consider leaving a review. Or, if you loved it, share it far and wide!

Now, on to the real reason for this author's note. When I wrote **Bite the Bullet** *(Bitten, #5)*, fans loved Rhys. They wondered if he was good or bad or if he would betray the five friends. I wasn't surprised because I loved him too. Who wouldn't adore a brooding, tortured soul like Rhys?

As I pondered his story, I realized he would need someone gentle but strong enough to relate to him. Someone who had suffered in a similar way. That's when I met Savannah. Yes, I say 'met' because the characters I write about feel real to me. Sometimes I have entire conversations with them in my head. Maybe that makes me weird, but it's part of how I write.

Savannah and Rhys wanted the same thing out of their lives—love. They wanted to be loved for who they were and to know that someone would be there for them, no matter what. They both deserved to get what they wanted.

When you finish this book, if you want a hint of what's to come next, check out my novella, **Destined by Blood**. There are two characters in the story that you might recognize...and it will tide you over until the final book in the Blood & Bone series is released this fall!

CHAPTER ONE

Rhys

THIS DAY WASN'T going as planned.

Tucking my hands in my pockets, I hunched my shoulders against the light rain that fell from the dull grey sky. After driving around with a realtor for the last three hours, I wasn't sure what I was going to do.

When I arrived in Austin months ago, I decided that I wanted to settle here. At least for a while. It would be the first time I had a home in centuries.

Places have a soul, just like people, and I felt a kinship with the spirit of this city.

I found a small rental home that suited me perfectly, but the landlord had recently given me notice that he needed the property back for his daughter who had just gotten married and was expecting his first grandchild. I couldn't blame him for wanting his family close. To help with my search for a new house, I contacted the real estate office I'd used previously. Although the agent I had worked with was no longer there, they assigned me a new one.

Unfortunately, the realtor didn't understand what I was looking for. My budget might be generous, but I had a vision of the home I wanted to live in and she couldn't seem to grasp that. Each house she showed me was larger than the one before. The last monstrosity she took me to was more of a palace than a home.

This was my second outing with the realtor and the time I'd wasted convinced me that she wasn't the right person to help me find what I was looking for. I was also beginning to wonder if perhaps this was a sign I should move on.

My chest tightened at the thought. I didn't want to move on. I liked it here. I felt more peace in the last few months than I had in hundreds of years. But fate was fickle and I'd learned the hard way not to ignore the small hints that the universe threw out.

The skies opened up and the light drizzle became a deluge. I dashed under an awning to escape the rain and noticed that I was standing in front of a coffee house. I smiled when I read the words on the window. *The Magic Bean.* The name was interesting and piqued my curiosity as to what might be inside. Suddenly, I was inundated with the desire for a cup of something hot. Opening the door, I stepped inside and found myself surrounded with warmth.

As I said before, places have a soul and the soul here was pure comfort. A smile tugged at the corner of my mouth and I moved deeper into the shop. The floors were dark wood and the walls were painted warm beige. The overall impression it created was cozy and calming. Small round tables stood toward the front of the store and an old wooden bar was fixed in the back left corner, polished to a bright sheen.

The smell of coffee and baked goods lingered in the air, but I could detect the underlying scent of oranges. My mouth watered as I walked toward the counter.

A blonde woman smiled at me from behind the bar, wiping her hands on a pristine white towel.

"Good morning," she greeted. "What can I get for you?"

I looked at the board on the wall behind her, studying the menu written in chalk. I didn't understand half of what was written there. Though I drank coffee, all the flavors and froth just confused me.

Before I could answer her question, she spoke again, "Would you trust me to choose something for you?" she asked.

Her words caught my attention. She was asking for my trust, something I didn't give easily. My gaze focused on her and I truly saw her for the first time. Her physical appearance was attractive, if relatively normal. She had long blonde hair and odd purple eyes that were an unsettling mixture of lavender and indigo. Then my sight went deeper. I realized that the homey feeling of the coffee shop reflected her. She was warmth and grace personified. Even from several feet away, I could feel the calming effects of her spirit.

The ability to see into the heart of a person was a by-product of all the things my maker had done to me. In moments like this, it came in handy. I might feed from the souls of others, but my predatory instincts knew who was trustworthy.

This woman was good to her core. Still, as I looked closer, there was a shadow around her, as though she were bound by something. Or someone.

"That sounds fine," I finally answered.

Her smile widened and I wondered if she knew how deeply I could read her. The thought was unsettling. Anonymity and ignorance were my only shields against enemies, known and unknown. She rang up my purchase, pausing to ask, "Would you like something to eat as well?"

I glanced into the glass case that sat atop the counter to my left and saw an assortment of pastries and other baked goods. To my right were three domed cake stands that held a cake and two variations of pie. That explained the smell that was making my mouth water.

"You choose," I told her, watching her closely.

Genuine delight radiated from the woman as she punched

more buttons on the tablet in front of her. "That will be seven dollars and fifty cents."

I fished my wallet out of my pocket and paid in cash, taking a moment to drop a couple of dollars into the ornate jar next to the register.

"Thanks," she said, clearly pleased with the tip. "Just grab a seat and I'll be with you in a moment."

I turned and realized that all the tables were surprisingly empty. It was rainy and cooler today than it had been during the weeks since I first arrived. The perfect day to linger in a shop over a steaming mug of coffee or tea and a book. Yet there was no one here.

Still, I was grateful for the solitude. Too much time around people made me twitchy. I'd spent centuries looking over my shoulder, always on edge around strangers. I never knew when a threat would make itself known. As a result, I tended to avoid places where people would congregate.

It wasn't until I settled into one of the booths that I realized that the other half of the shop held merchandise. There were two large circular tables near the front of the space that were littered with hunks of crystals and rocks, jewelry, and odds and ends. Shelves holding books and candles ran along the walls and jutted out into the center of the store. There was a small niche at the rear, opposite the coffee bar. Instead of a door, the little room was separated from the rest of the floor by heavy velvet curtains in dark green. The curtains were drawn back to reveal an antique round table of dark wood with a matching chair on each side.

I wasn't sure what purpose the room served, but I could feel the faint pulse of magic emanating from it. Now that I was seated and attuned to the store, I realized that magic was woven into the very building that surrounded me. It was so subtle that I hadn't noticed it when I first walked in, but I suddenly sensed it clearly.

When the woman from the counter walked up to the table, holding a large mug and saucer and a plate with two pastries stacked on it, I studied her. It was as if a veil had been lifted and I could see the power that emanated from her. It twisted and writhed beneath the shadow that shrouded her, as though it yearned to be free.

She was a witch.

In my extremely long life, I'd never liked witches. Considering a warlock had made me what I am, my experience with them hadn't been the best up until I met one in Dallas who was truly a white witch. It didn't change my opinion of them as a whole, but it did force me to consider that there were others that were also kind.

The blonde witch standing before me was compassionate and welcoming. Though she would probably deny it, she was also strong. Strong enough to fight any battles that came her way, which made the shadow that surrounded her even more mysterious and interesting.

She smiled a little as she set the drink and plate of food on the table in front of me. "Vanilla bourbon latte, a blueberry orange scone, and a chocolate oatmeal Scotchie."

I stared down into the drink, hesitant to try it. I rarely drank spirits, preferring to keep my wits about me. "It has bourbon in it?"

"Just a flavored syrup, no alcohol," she replied, her grin growing wider.

Still unsure, I lifted the cup to my lips, inhaling the scent of coffee and vanilla with a whiff of something stronger. When I sipped, I couldn't hide my surprise, my eyebrows lifting. "That's delicious," I complimented her.

She laughed and sat down across from me. "Thank you."

Her behavior was not what I'd come to expect from employees at restaurants and coffee houses. But the shop was empty, so I couldn't blame her for wanting to take a break.

"That room," I said, gesturing toward the curtained niche. "What is it for?"

"It's where Savannah or I do tarot card readings, palmistry, and other types of divination."

"Really?" I asked.

"Yes."

My eyes moved over the shelves of books and candles then to the tables at the front of the store that held crystals and amulets. "And you sell other magical aids and items." It was a declaration not a question.

"I do." She held her hand out across the table. "I'm Ava Amaris."

"Hello, Ava. My name is Rhys Carey."

"Hi, Rhys. What brings you into my shop on this dreary day?" she asked.

"This is your shop?" I responded, evading her curious gaze as I sipped the latte.

Ava nodded, her purple eyes sparkling with mischief. "It is. But you still haven't answered my question."

Since she wasn't going to let it go, I answered, "I was in the area, looking at houses with a realtor."

"Oh, are you moving to Austin?"

I hesitated. "You're asking a lot of questions to a stranger," I stated bluntly.

She laughed. "I am, aren't I? I've always been nosy." Ava rested her elbows on the table and leaned forward. "But I don't just own this store. I also own several homes that I rent out. I might be able to help you."

I picked up the cookie and took a bite as I considered her words. The flavors of chocolate and butterscotch exploded on my tongue. When my eyes widened in shock, she laughed again, the sound light and clear.

"Did you make this?" I asked.

"I did. I make all my baked goods."

"It's amazing."

"Thank you," she replied.

As I chewed and swallowed the cookie, I made a decision. This witch had a bright light within her, a light of goodness and generosity. Plus she baked delicious cookies. "Do you have a house to rent now?"

She beamed at me. "I do. It's not large or fancy, but it is homey."

"I'd be interested in seeing it," I said.

"No problem. Let me get you the key. You'll be able to walk there. It's only two blocks away."

She disappeared into the rear of the shop for a few moments, returning with a silver key dangling from her fingertips. She hesitated as she held it out to me, murmuring a few quiet words over the key.

"What was that?" I asked as I felt a small burst of magic from her.

Ava grinned mischievously. "Just making sure that you can't leave until you return my key."

"You aren't coming?"

Ava shook her head. "No. I can't leave the shop." Her head cocked. "I also think it's best if you see the house by yourself.

When my fingers closed around the key, my blood sang as power vibrated between us. I nearly dropped the ring, but managed to maintain my hold. I looked up and saw that Ava was watching me closely, as her eyes shifted from dark indigo to a lighter shade of violet. Her skin grew luminous, as though the shadow that surrounded her could no longer contain the glow of her power. It was as if the light within her soul was suddenly visible.

"I'm glad your journey brought you here, Rhys."

I stared at her in confusion. As abruptly as it began, the swell of magic between us vanished. The glow of Ava's skin faded and her eyes returned to the strange mix purple and blue they were before.

"Now, let me write down the address and directions to the house and you can go take a look," she stated, releasing the end of the key ring which made me jerk slightly. I hadn't realized she was still holding it.

As SOON AS I stopped in front of the address, I knew I'd found the place I was searching for. The house was small, blue, and trimmed in white, with a nearly non-existent yard.

I moved up the front walk and climbed the steps to the covered porch. Fitting the key into the lock, I turned the knob and hesitated when I heard a light sigh. When I looked around, I was alone.

Still unsure, I slowly pushed the door open, wondering if the house truly was empty. As I stepped over the threshold, I felt the pulse of power and realized that the sigh I'd heard was a spell. The magic faded as I walked deeper into the room, shutting the door behind me.

I looked around at the living room, surprised to see it was furnished with a worn beige sofa and oversized armchair. A small kitchen stood to the left, the appliances old but well-maintained. The house smelled of lemons, as though it had just been cleaned. As though Ava expected me.

Curious, I moved down the hall. On each side of the hallway, there was an open door. I glanced in each room and found them both empty. One was a bit larger than the other and I immediately decided that it would be my bedroom. Another door lay at the end of the hall and when I opened it, I found a tidy bathroom. The fixtures were newer than those in the kitchen and the tiles sparkled.

The same warmth and generosity I felt from Ava radiated throughout the house. Just like her coffee shop, *The Magic Bean*.

I decided then and there that this place would be my home. At least for the next few months. Something inside me shifted and settled, the constant tension in my muscles eased somewhat. I wasn't completely relaxed, but it was enough.

As I stepped out of the house and locked the door, the sun came out from behind the clouds, glinting off something across the street. My eyes caught on the yard opposite mine. A gnarled tree hid one side of the house, but I could clearly see that it looked like a small stone cottage, an odd addition to this neighborhood. The rest of the front yard was filled with flowers and plants, but in a wild explosion rather than an orderly fashion. The effect was chaotic but charming. Oddly, I almost expected to see fairies zipping around among the blossoms.

Another flash of light caught my eye and I realized the sun was reflecting off a delicate set of metal wind chimes. Hanging motionless from the branch, they gleamed brightly in the rays. A larger set of wooden wind chimes dangled nearby as well, but neither of the chimes so much as swayed.

As I set off down the sidewalk back to the coffee shop, I wondered what sort of person lived in a fairytale cottage and took the time to create a whimsical garden despite the amount of upkeep it had to require.

Considering we were about to become neighbors, I was certain I would soon find out.

CHAPTER TWO

Savannah

I OPENED THE door to *The Magic Bean* and the scent of freshly brewed espresso immediately washed over me.

"Good morning!" Ava called from behind the counter.

"It's too early for you to be so cheerful," I grumbled beneath my breath.

"What was that?"

I approached the counter, moving around to join Ava behind it. "It's too darn early for you to be so cheerful," I repeated, raising my voice a little.

Ava smirked at me as she handed me a cup and saucer, the froth on top decorated in a pretty design. I figured it was witchcraft because no matter how much I practiced, I could never get any design I tried to turn out right.

"You are a goddess," I breathed, accepting the cup and lifting it up to take a whiff. The perfume of espresso, vanilla, and bourbon hit my nose, perking me up. "Why do we have to open at the crack of dawn anyway?" I asked her after I took a sip.

"Because most people like to drink coffee in the morning, not at noon," she replied, going back to the antique glass case to finish arranging the pastries and scones inside.

"Any true coffee lover drinks it any time." I set the cup to the side and stowed my purse beneath the counter. As I pulled my apron from its hook on the wall, I glanced around the store. "Um, there's no one here now."

"That's because it's after eight. The worst of the morning rush is over."

I scoffed and picked up my latte. I wanted to give her a hard time for having me come in when she clearly didn't need me, but I wouldn't. Ava was my boss and my landlord, but most important-ly, she was my friend. Even though I had to be awake earlier in the day than I liked, I still enjoyed spending time with her.

Ava Amaris saved me from myself. When I met her ten years ago, she took one look at the trembling wreck that I was and held out her hand. She was an exemplary woman. She was also the easiest person for me to be around. With my condition, I found proximity to people for prolonged periods to be exhausting and wrenching. The constant bombardment of emotions, the minute changes in mood that accompanied everyday life, they wore me down.

Not with Ava. I'd known as soon as I met her that she was much more than an exceptional person. She was magical. In the literal sense. It hadn't taken me long to see that there was more to Ava Amaris than met the eye.

Her emotions and her moods were never overwhelming. She soothed me. I knew that part of the reason we fit so well together was because she wasn't a typical human.

"Also, I wanted to tell you about your new neighbor."

That got my attention. "What? Neighbor?"

She smiled as she closed the glass case, brushing her hands over her apron. "Yeah. A man rented my house across the street from you. Haven't you seen him?"

I shook my head and drank more coffee. "When did he move in?" I asked, curious about him.

"Last week. Surely there was a moving truck."

I shrugged. "I don't know. I never saw one."

"Strange," she murmured.

I waited for her to elaborate but she remained silent, using a clean, damp towel to wipe down the counter. "Why is it strange? And don't think I don't know what you're doing."

"Hm?" She hummed in the back of her throat, her face the picture of utter innocence, which immediately made me even more suspicious.

I squinted at her. "I know what your game is, Ava. You brought him up for a reason."

"Well, he's single and new in town." She stopped speaking, but I waited. "He's…different."

"Different?"

"Like you and me. He has power."

"Oh." I wasn't sure what to make of that. In my experience, most supernatural beings avoided me. Secrets, thoughts, even emotions were carefully guarded in this community. Knowledge like that could be dangerous for magical creatures of any kind.

Ava glanced at me, her expression wry. "No need to be worried, Savannah. I'm only mentioning it because he could use a friend and I didn't want you to be surprised the first time you met him."

"Well, if he's been living there a week, I probably should have seen him by now. I've been in the front garden every day."

Ava didn't say another word, her focus on the counter she was wiping down.

I drained my latte. "You didn't tell me much else about him. Is he younger, older? A warlock?"

"He looks young," she answered cryptically.

I studied Ava, reading between the lines. "Appearances can be deceiving."

We exchanged a glance. I wasn't sure exactly how old Ava was, but I knew she hadn't aged a day in ten years. She still looked about twenty-five years old. The weight behind her emotions told me more about her true age than her appearance. Though she shared pieces of her past on rare occasions, I could feel how each experience had left its mark on her psyche.

"He's lonely," she stated quietly.

I bit my bottom lip and looked down at the counter, something twisting inside my belly. I knew the feeling of loneliness all too well. Empathy welled within me that had nothing to do with another person's emotions and everything to do with my own. "I'll stop by and introduce myself," I stated.

She smiled. "Good. I have a feeling you two will hit it off."

Immediately, I knew she was up to something, but the door to the shop opened before I could reply. I decided to let the matter drop. Just because she wanted to play matchmaker didn't mean that I had to comply.

A FEW HOURS later, I leaned a hip against the counter and rubbed my aching temples. I took slow, deep breaths, focusing on inhaling and exhaling as my head throbbed. The shop had been surprisingly busy all morning. A steady stream of witches and warlocks came through the doors for coffee and supplies for potions and spells. Most of them were skilled enough that their mental blocks were strong, but there was still a constant buzz of emotions all around me. It was exhausting and it had finally caught up with me.

To my relief, the flow of people slowed until the shop was empty. Ava glanced at the clock then at me.

"It's two. Go ahead and go home. Spend some time in your garden, maybe take a nap." I started to argue, but she lifted a hand.

"You're a part-time employee and your boss is telling you to go home."

I relented because the pressure behind my eyes grew with each passing moment. All I wanted to do was close the blackout drapes in my bedroom and crawl into bed. It would be stupid to argue about this when it was what I needed anyway. "Fine, but I'll be back tomorrow afternoon."

"You'll do tarot readings tomorrow and that's it," she said firmly.

I took off my apron and hung it from the hook. Ava and I could have this out tomorrow when I was fresh and not wishing for a bottle of ibuprofen and a dark room.

"See you tomorrow," I said.

"Go home and rest," Ava replied, giving me a squinty look that said she didn't believe I truly would.

"I will," I promised, utterly sincere.

I stepped out of the shop and hissed as the sunlight hit my eyes. Quickly, I dug my dark sunglasses out of my bag and slipped them on. Grateful that the house I rented from Ava was close by, I focused on putting one foot in front of the other and headed home.

Though her bossiness was sometimes annoying, I adored Ava. I knew she had my best interest at heart. I might have been able to get by without her help and her presence, but my life would have been far emptier. My grandmother left me a small inheritance that would pay my bills if I lived frugally. But I needed a job for more than money. Even though the emotions of others were difficult to take on a regular basis, being around people helped dispel the excruciating loneliness. Being an empath, I required a great deal of isolation to recover from any kind of social situation, but as a human being, I still needed friends and conversation. Chatting online was nice, but it didn't replace the need to look into another person's face and share a meal.

It also didn't replace physical contact. Despite the pain it might cause me to be in the presence of others, I loved to be touched. Not necessarily in a sexual way, though that was something I missed as well, but just a quick hug or holding hands. Even an absent caress on my arm or leg. I craved the contact.

As I walked home, the beautiful spring day soothed the frayed edges of my spirit and eased the pain in my head, but it didn't lift my mood. Talking about my new neighbor with Ava had brought my own loneliness to the forefront. I knew she'd intentionally brought up his seclusion because she wanted me to empathize with him but it also highlighted my own issues.

I loved Ava like a sister, but the woman knew exactly which buttons to press when she wanted me to do something. She tended to push me when I needed it and the outcome was usually for the best. I would never admit that to her because she was already convinced she knew what was best for everyone. There was no need to feed her ego. She was bossy enough as it was.

Even though I knew that Ava had an ulterior motive, she accomplished her goal anyway. As I approached my house, I looked across the street at the little blue cottage Ava also owned, thinking about who might be inside. It had been vacant for the past few months and I'd wondered if she even wanted to find a tenant.

It was strange that I'd never seen the man who rented it, even in passing. I spent a lot of time outside in the front garden. I should have at least caught a glimpse of him coming or going, maybe getting his mail, but I hadn't. As far as I could tell, the house still appeared vacant.

I hesitated on my front porch, my eyes scanning the structure across the street. Then I decided to do something impulsive, even though I was tired. If I hadn't seen my neighbor, then he probably hadn't left the house much since he moved in. The thought made something in my belly twist again. I hated the idea of someone feeling the same loneliness I did when I could do something to dispel it.

I went inside the house and grabbed my shears. I would take my new neighbor a bouquet of flowers from my garden to welcome him. Then I wouldn't spend most of the evening mulling over Ava's words about his isolation and feeling as though I should do something about it.

CHAPTER THREE

Rhys

THE DOORBELL RANG. At least I thought it was the doorbell. I'd never lived in a home that had one before.

Putting aside the book I'd purchased at the shop down the street, I got to my feet, went to the door, and put my eye to the peephole. Even though Cornelius had been dead for nearly a year now, my suspicious tendencies had yet to be broken.

A woman stood on the porch, her head bowed. All I could see was a tumble of dark brown hair and a bundle of flowers clutched in her hands.

Sensing no danger, I unlocked the door. Her head lifted as the door swung open and I stopped moving as surprise washed over me. I could see her aura. Despite my abilities to see into the spirit of a person, I very rarely saw auras. Every person I'd met who had a visible aura had been remarkable in some way or another.

Good or evil, their abilities or personality were stronger than a typical human's.

However, I had never seen an aura like hers before. White light radiated around her body, shot through with threads in a rainbow of colors, as though she experienced every emotion simultaneously. Except around her head. Shades of grey, brown, and black surrounded her skull like a halo. Thin strips of red shimmered among the darkness. She was in pain. For some reason that realization upset me. I didn't like the idea of this woman hurting in any way.

My eyes focused on her face and very little of that discomfort showed in her expression. Her brown eyes were wide, staring back at me in surprise, but she recovered quickly.

"Uh, hi, my name is Savannah Baker. I live across the street. I work for Ava and she mentioned that you moved in, so I thought I would introduce myself. I mean, she suggested that I introduce myself because you just moved here and you haven't had a chance to make friends yet." Her eyes widened again and a bright pink flush spread intriguingly from her cheeks down her neck, to cover the skin of her chest that was exposed by the slim straps of her dress. My eyes wanted to linger on the vee neckline as I wondered exactly how far down the blush extended, but the choked sound she made caught my attention. "And I'm babbling. I'm sorry."

Savannah lifted the bouquet toward me. "Anyway, I just wanted to bring you some flowers from my garden as sort of a welcome to the neighborhood."

I stared blankly at the colorful explosion of blooms she held out for a moment and then realized I was supposed to take it. I lifted my hands, my fingertips brushing hers as I took possession of the glass vase she held.

She made another sound, almost a squeak, and released the vase before I held it securely. Quickly, I grabbed the glass before it crashed to the porch, droplets of water splashing my hands and forearms.

"Oh, my God, I'm sorry," she groaned. "I'm glad you caught that." Savannah hesitated, cleared her throat, and gestured to the house opposite us. "Anyway, I live right across the street. If you need anything or want someone to show you around, feel free to knock on my door any time."

I studied her face as another brilliant blush washed over her pale skin, highlighting the freckles on her nose and cheeks. She lowered her lashes, shielding her eyes from me. Immediately I felt the loss of her gaze, which also surprised me. I liked the idea of her eyes on mine. I wanted her to look at me again and never look away. I inhaled sharply at the thought. Determined, I shook it off and studied the small woman standing on my porch.

Now that I was no longer dumbstruck by her aura, I noticed that Savannah Baker was a very pretty woman. Her dark hair flowed down her back in long waves and the freckles that dotted her cheeks were also visible on her chest and shoulders as well. The loose dress she wore hid most of her figure and legs, but I could see the curves of her breasts and hips beneath the material and I knew she would be soft in all the right places.

The sudden rush of attraction took me by surprise. It had been a long time since I'd felt anything other than tepid interest in a woman.

"Okay, so it was nice to meet you and I'm just gonna go," she murmured, stepping back.

My first instinct was to stop her. I didn't want her to leave. I opened my mouth to ask her to stay, to come inside, but she kept speaking.

"I hope you enjoy the house. Ava is a really good landlord. I've been renting from her for a few years. If you have any problems, just give her a call and she'll get them taken care of quickly. Enjoy the flowers."

With that, she turned and scurried down the steps as I stood frozen on the porch, still holding the flowers aloft. I could hear her muttering beneath her breath as she walked away and it sounded as if she said, "Way to make an idiot of yourself, Savannah."

It wasn't until she'd crossed the street and disappeared into her own house that I realized I hadn't spoken a single word the entire time she'd been here. She likely thought I was rude or peculiar.

I carried the flowers inside and shut the front door. I wanted to walk across the street and tell her my name. I wanted to talk to her longer, learn more about her. I wanted her to look at me again because, with her eyes on me, I felt as though someone was truly seeing me for the first time. Savannah Baker interested me more than any other person I'd met in a few decades.

Strangely, I was unsure what to do. I avoided people, even women. The need to feed was the only reason I would bother to talk to anyone, and even then I chose those who carried excess pain or torment. This was an alien situation.

Feeding was always a tricky process. Gaius had made me into a vampire of sorts. I needed to feed off the very life force of a person rather than their blood. Essentially, devouring their soul. Cornelius, my brother, would consume a soul in its entirety. He believed it gave him greater power. He was right, but it increased his madness and deepened his conviction that he could become a god among humans and supernatural creatures alike.

I discovered long ago that feeding from the pain of others would keep me alive. It wasn't as potent, but it kept me from fading away. It also relieved the suffering of my victim. Yes, even though I hoped to help them, I still considered the people I fed from to be my victims. Emotional vampirism was still an invasion, still a theft of life force.

By choosing those who were in agony, I could live with what I did. I was probably deluding myself, but it helped me come to terms with what I was. What I still am. Not completely human, yet not the monster my brother had become. No, I was a monster of a different sort.

Moving slowly, I carried the flowers into the living room and set them on the table in front of the chair I'd been sitting in earlier. I sat down and stared at the colorful blooms. They reminded me of Savannah's aura. Every color of the rainbow was represented and they were vibrant, almost shimmering with life.

A strange sensation settled in my chest, a heaviness that made it difficult to breathe. I needed to avoid Savannah Baker, regardless of how interesting I found her. It was for the best.

CHAPTER FOUR

Savannah

A S I WALKED home, I berated myself under my breath. I couldn't believe I'd acted like such an idiot. My only defense was that my new neighbor had the kind of good looks that rendered even the brightest woman utterly brainless.

It was a new experience for me. Most of my interactions with people were based on their emotions rather than their appearance. I always felt their mood before I even saw their face.

That hadn't been the case with him. As soon as he opened the door, all I saw was his broad shoulders, beautiful face, and dark blond hair. I'd barely registered that his eyes were odd at the time, completely black as though the pupil had swallowed the iris. Which was weird. I shook off the peculiar thought. It was likely his eyes were just a very dark brown. When he stepped out onto the porch, I'd caught a whiff of his cologne or soap or whatever he used and nearly dropped the flowers I'd been holding out to him.

My new neighbor was stupid hot. As in, so hot it made me stupid.

I'd been so busy babbling that he hadn't had time to reply to anything I said. I hadn't even given him a chance to tell me his name! Though I doubted I would be using it anytime soon. If ever. My stupid hot neighbor would probably avoid me as often as possible. It was clear that he was already a loner.

When I went back inside the house, I crept to the window and glanced outside, torturing myself a little because I hoped he might be lingering on his porch. I shrank back from the window when I saw that he was indeed still standing in the same spot where I left him, staring at my house and holding the flowers I'd given him as though he couldn't decide whether to toss them in the yard or carry them inside.

I groaned and leaned my back against the wall next to the window, sliding down until my rear end hit the floor.

"Could I be any more awkward?" I asked my empty living room.

My cat, Satchel, meowed as she came around the corner and made a beeline for me. She butted her head against my hand and meowed again, demanding that I pet her. I sighed and ran my hand over her head gently, stroking her soft grey fur.

"Hey, Satchel," I cooed.

The look she shot me clearly showed her disdain for her name. Then she plopped down on the floor and began to lick her paw. Somehow she managed to make the feline gesture look imperious. Her demeanor was more suited to a moniker like Anastasia or Elizabeth, but the night I'd found her in the street she'd been so bedraggled and scrawny that she fit perfectly in my small bag. Hence the name Satchel.

"Mommy made a fool of herself in front of her sexy new neighbor," I told her.

I knew that cats couldn't roll their eyes, but Satchel came close. She gave me a look of disgust and trotted off toward the back of the house. Obviously, she felt no sympathy for my plight.

With a sigh, I heaved myself to my feet, rubbing my butt with one hand as the numbness gave way to prickles of pins and needles. I needed to get some exercise if sitting on my floor was enough to put my rear end to sleep.

The headache that I'd successfully ignored all afternoon reared its ugly head once again. The dull ache sharpened into a hot, piercing pain just behind my left eye. I stumbled back to my bedroom, kicking off my shoes before I stretched out on the bed. The room was blessedly cool and dark, so I closed my eyes and focused on my breathing.

Maybe after my nap I would feel better. Or maybe I would wake up and the entire humiliating experience with my neighbor would be a dream. I smiled a little. That would be nice. Maybe then I would have an opportunity to talk to him again without the babbling and awkwardness.

I settled deeper into the mattress and felt Satchel's weight hit the bed a few seconds before she curled up into the small of my back. Despite her haughty attitude, she really was a sweet cat. She seemed to sense when I was having a rough day and would often offer me comfort.

With her warm, minute weight resting against me, I fell asleep.

THE SOUND OF the phone ringing woke me. Still half asleep, I fumbled for the receiver and lifted it to my ear.

"Lo?" I mumbled.

"Are you still sleeping?" Ava asked. "It's nearly seven."

I winced. I hadn't meant to sleep so late, but I hadn't set an alarm on my cell phone to wake me up. "Well, I'm up now."

"So did you go see my new tenant today?"

I rolled over onto my back and rubbed my forehead. The headache behind my eyes had disappeared, but my embarrassment hadn't. "Yeah," I sighed.

"Uh-oh, that doesn't sound good," she murmured. "What happened?"

"Well, for one thing, you didn't warn me how hot he was," I accused her. "I could have prepared myself. Or stayed home. Instead I sounded like a babbling idiot. Oh, and I nearly dropped a vase of flowers on his foot, which thankfully he caught. Unfortunately, in catching the vase, he was also splashed with water."

Ava laughed and I made a face at the phone. "I'm sorry, Savannah. I'm not laughing at you."

Rolling my eyes, I replied, "Yeah, I can tell you're laughing with me."

Still giggling, she continued, "I didn't think he was *that* good looking."

I wasn't ready to let go of my humiliation. "Make an appointment with an eye doctor. I'm concerned that your vision is going."

Ava laughed harder. "Okay, so he's handsome. Did he render you speechless?"

"No, the exact opposite. I had verbal diarrhea. It was so embarrassing. I didn't even stop talking long enough for him to tell me his name. I went over there to welcome him to the neighborhood and I still don't know his name!" I exclaimed, covering my eyes with my free hand at the memory. "Who does that?"

"Apparently, you do," Ava answered.

"Please stop trying to make me feel better. You suck at it."

"Then maybe I need more practice," she retorted.

I groaned.

"Savannah, I'm sure you're overreacting to the situation. Think about it. Did you sense irritation or disgust from him when you were talking?"

I froze then as an epiphany hit me so hard that it nearly hurt. "No."

"See? He wasn't–"

"No, Ava. You don't understand. I felt *nothing* from him. No emotion at all. He was completely blank." My heart raced. I'd never experienced anything like that before. I hadn't even sensed his mental barriers. Even when I couldn't feel Ava's emotions or those of the witches I met from time to time, I could sense their mental walls. I knew they were there, almost as if I could see them. With my new neighbor, there was nothing. Just silence and stillness.

She fell quiet for a long moment. "Really?"

"Yeah. It was like he didn't have emotions at all. Or his mental shields are as solid as a concrete wall three feet thick and completely invisible to me."

"That's probably it," she replied. "I don't know a lot about him, but I can tell he's had a long, difficult life."

"And his eyes." I trailed off then.

"What about them?"

"They were black."

I could practically feel the change in Ava's mood vibrate through the phone. "What? I never noticed that."

"It was strange," I mused. "I felt like he could see right through me."

"Okay, that's it. I'm coming over. You're going to tell me exactly what happened and then I need to make a decision."

"About what?" I asked in confusion.

"About whether Rhys stays or goes."

"His name's Rhys?"

"Yes, his name's Rhys, but that's not what's important right now."

She clearly knew something I didn't. "What's important, Ava?" I questioned, my eyes narrowing. "Why are you talking about making him leave?"

"Your safety."

"Well, that's a bit melodramatic, don't you think?" His emotions were a blank slate to me, but he didn't seem dangerous.

"We'll see," she replied mysteriously. "I'll be there in half an hour."

She disconnected the call before I could respond.

I was pacing by the door when Ava pulled up in front of the house. I forced myself to wait until she knocked before I opened the door and pulled her inside.

"Whoa, calm down," she said, juggling two bottles of wine and a plastic bag full of food.

"Calm down? You make some cryptic statement that implies I may not be safe, hang up on me, and then have the nerve to tell me to calm down? Are you crazy?" My voice rose as I spoke until I was nearly yelling.

"Yes, calm down," Ava repeated. "I don't think he's going to come over here and murder us with an axe."

"What a relief," I shot back, throwing my hands up in the air. "Do you think he'll use his bare hands?"

Ava shook her head. "Stop being a drama queen and help me carry this stuff into the kitchen."

I took the bottles of wine she held out to me and followed her to the rear of the house where the kitchen was located. I put one of the bottles in my fridge and set about opening the other as Ava unpacked the food.

"I'm sorry if I freaked you out," she apologized. "I don't think Rhys truly means anyone harm. I was just surprised that you didn't feel any emotion from him. You're one of the strongest empaths I've ever met so I didn't expect you to tell me that he was blank to you." She took a plate from the cabinet, opened a wheel of Brie, and began peeling the wrapper off the cheese. "Now that I've taken the time to think about it, it makes sense. Like I said, I got the impression his life hasn't been easy. In fact, I'm pretty sure it's been hellish. A man like that will have stone walls for mental barriers. Or magical protection. He couldn't risk having someone pluck the thoughts from his mind."

I grabbed two wineglasses and poured us each a generous measure of chilled white wine. Her words made sense. Maybe Rhys used his power to protect his thoughts and feelings. "Okay, so you're saying you overreacted?"

"Of course not," she disagreed.

I finished pouring wine and stared at her.

"Maybe a little," she admitted. "Still, I want you to tell me exactly what happened and then I'll be certain if I overreacted or not."

I handed her one of the wineglasses and snatched a cracker from the plate she was arranging.

"Hey, you're messing up my pretty plate here."

"It's going to get really messed up in a minute when we sit down to eat it. What does it matter?"

She sighed and didn't say anything else when I snagged a gherkin from the pile she'd just scooped onto the plate. I watched as she finished portioning out crackers, cheese, pickles, and pate. Now that I had food in front of me, I was ravenous.

"Let's go into the living room and you can tell me everything."

We settled on my sofa and I told her about how I babbled and how Rhys didn't say a word the entire time I was there. I finished up with explaining how his eyes had been completely black and he was an emotional blank slate.

When I was done, I wasn't sure which freaked me out more—the fact that I embarrassed myself in front of him or that he was an emotional null.

I drained my wineglass and waited. Oddly, Ava had nothing to say. I poured more wine and munched on crackers and cheese.

Finally I couldn't take her silence any longer. "Well, what do you think?"

She stared at me, but her eyes were unfocused as though she was looking beyond me, and I could practically see the gears turning in her mind. "About what?"

"About Rhys!" I replied, my voice loud.

Ava blinked and suddenly seemed to return to the present. "I think that you have nothing to worry about," she stated. "I also think that he's as rusty around people as you are."

That definitely didn't make me feel any better. I didn't say anything else, mostly because I didn't want to verbalize how much I was obsessing over my encounter with him. Instead, I went back to eating and drinking wine. Ava and I chatted about the coffee shop and the clients that came in for regular tarot readings, but let the subject of Rhys drop.

It wasn't until I stood up to carry our empty plates into the kitchen that I realized I was more than a little tipsy from all the wine I'd drunk. As I rinsed the plates and loaded them into the dishwasher, Ava followed me into the kitchen and opened the second bottle of wine she brought.

We drifted back into the living room and resumed our positions on the couch. When I curled up against the cushions, Satchel appeared, hopped up into my lap, and settled down with a contented purr as I stroked her back.

Pleasant warmth suffused my body as the wine seeped into my bloodstream. My mind drifted back to what I'd been mulling over on my walk home and how her earlier description of Rhys and his isolation reminded me of myself. Without thinking, I asked Ava, "Do you ever get lonely?"

She blinked at me for a moment, her face expressionless. "Sometimes, I guess."

I sighed, slumping down in the cushions a little more. "I do. I'm lonely all the time."

"You have me," she replied softly. "And other friends."

Smiling at her, I touched her hand where it rested along the back of the couch. "I do. I'm so glad you're my friend." My eyes stung and I blinked rapidly, wondering why I suddenly felt like crying. "I guess I just mean I'm lonely for…male companionship."

Ava chuckled. "You mean sex?" she asked before sipping her wine.

"That's part of it, yes. But there's more. I just want someone," I paused. "A man, here. I want someone to share my life with. You are wonderful and I love you, but I want my other half. I need him." I sighed again, sinking deeper into the maudlin mood that had come over me. "I know it's not very modern or feminist of me, but I want someone to love and who loves me in return. I want weeknight dinners, bickering, and Sunday mornings in bed."

"It sounds like you want an ordinary relationship, the kind that millions of people have," Ava pointed out.

"Don't you see?" I asked her. "With the right person, ordinary becomes extraordinary. Vital and necessary."

Ava responded, but I could barely hear her. My head bobbed forward and I jerked it up. She laughed. "I think you've had a little too much wine," she stated, reaching out to take my glass from me. "Let's get you to bed."

I let her help me to my feet and lead me back to my bedroom. "I want my extraordinary normal," I murmured.

"I know, sweetie," Ava whispered. "I want that for you too."

CHAPTER FIVE

Rhys

As I walked to *The Magic Bean*, I told myself it was because I wanted a latte and pastries and not to assuage my curiosity about Savannah. It wasn't until I turned the corner and stopped in front of the shop that I gave up the pretense.

Since she brought me flowers yesterday, I found that my mind wandered back to her again and again. I wanted to see her and actually talk to her instead of standing across from her and staring at her like a brainless oaf. While I was curious about her aura and the rainbow of colors she radiated, there was more to it than that. I was drawn to her, more than any other woman I'd ever met. Even after the short, one-sided conversation yesterday, I couldn't stop thinking about her.

When I opened the door to the shop, the scents of coffee and orange wafted out. My mouth watered. I stepped inside and immediately saw Ava behind the counter, smiling at a customer. When her eyes came to me, her smile widened.

"Rhys! It's great to see you. Do you want something to drink?"

The customer moved on, carrying a steaming mug to a table. I nodded as I approached the counter. "I liked that latte you made me before."

"Do you want something to eat?" she asked.

"Not right now, thanks."

I glanced around the shop as she made my drink, surreptitiously looking for Savannah.

She set the cup in front of me and took my money, her purple eyes gleaming with mischief. I was beginning to think it was her default expression. "Are you looking for Savannah?" Her voice was low.

I wanted to deny it, but it was obvious that the witch could see right through me. "Is she here?"

Ava tilted her head toward the niche where she said they did tarot readings and I noticed that the curtains were closed. "She's doing a reading, but she should be done in a few minutes. She'll be free for a bit after that." The witch studied me for a moment. "How do you like the house?"

"It's comfortable," I replied, taking a drink from the latte. Flavors burst into my mouth and I immediately took another.

The corner of her mouth hiked up. "Just comfortable?"

I shrugged. "I think that's the most important aspect of any home, don't you?"

Ava tilted her head, her eyes narrowing on me. "That's a good point. Is the garage big enough for your car?"

"I don't have a car," I replied, draining the last of my cup.

"You don't have a car?" Her voice rose as she spoke.

I shrugged. "I don't really need one."

"How do you get from one place to another? Or go to the grocery store?"

I looked around, but no one appeared to be paying attention to our conversation. Leaning forward, I answered, "I either walk or use magic."

Her eyebrows lifted. "You can trace?"

I nodded. The ability to utilize magic to teleport wasn't common in the supernatural community, but I'd been able to do it since Gaius made me. I found that it came in handy when I needed to get from one place to another quickly. Or to escape my enemies.

"Interesting," she murmured. "But don't people notice that or think it's strange that you don't have a vehicle?"

I glanced at her. I'd never thought of that before. "I don't know. I don't spend much time around other people."

Ava smiled slyly. "If you're serious about fitting in with society, you should definitely consider getting one. If you know how to drive, that is."

"I've never driven a vehicle before, but it doesn't seem that difficult."

Ava's eyes widened. "It's not really, but it is something that requires practice."

I mulled over her words. I'd never considered purchasing a car before because my energy would have prevented it from running. Something about my power disrupted electrical currents. Until a few months ago. Kerry, the white witch I knew, had sent me an amulet. It contained powerful, old magic and made it possible for me to interact with the world. Now I could watch television, talk on the phone, and ride in a vehicle without causing them to smoke or catch fire. Maybe it was time for me to acquire a more tradition-al means of transportation.

The sound of the curtain being pulled back drew my attention. I looked over my shoulder and saw Savannah walking out of the niche with an older woman. The woman's hand rested on Savan-nah's forearm and Savannah's palm curved over her fingers. Speaking softly to her, Savannah walked the woman out the door.

"You should have Savannah give you a reading," Ava suggest-ed. "She's very good with the cards."

I glanced at her. "She's a witch?" That could explain her aura.

Ava shook her head. "Not exactly. She's an empath, but with extra abilities." She smiled. "I've never met another person like

Savannah. She's everything that's gentle and good."

I understood then what I saw in Savannah's aura. She was a receptor for emotions. She appeared to experience every emotion at once because she received them all.

"Look, go sit down in the reading room and I'll send her in when she comes back," Ava directed.

Instead of refusing once again, my feet carried me toward the room. After I settled in one of the chairs, Ava pulled the curtains closed to separate me from the rest of the shop. As I waited, I wondered what I was doing. Divination of any kind wasn't something I put stock in. Cards, numbers, palms, none of that could tell me what the future held. Destiny was a changeable entity, practically a living thing. To believe that it could be predicted struck me as ludicrous.

The longer I sat in the chair, the more uncomfortable I felt. Just as I was about to get to my feet and leave the room, the curtain swept back to reveal Savannah.

She froze for a moment when she saw me, her eyes wide. Recovering quickly, she stepped inside the niche and let the fabric fall behind her.

"Good afternoon," she greeted me. "It's nice to see you again, Rhys."

While her expression appeared serene, that becoming flush I'd noticed yesterday returned to her cheeks and neck. I could also see the changes in her aura. She was embarrassed for some reason. She was also feeling attraction. I could only assume it was for me since I was the only other person in the room. I took satisfaction in that knowledge because it meant I wasn't the only one who felt the pull between us.

Intrigued, I immediately decided to stay and see what else I could learn about Savannah Baker.

"Hi, Savannah," I replied.

The pink in her cheeks darkened further. "What brings you to the shop today?"

"I came for coffee and Ava suggested I get a reading."

Savannah sat on the chair across from me, perching as though she were a mere second from taking flight. "Do you often practice forms of divination?"

I cleared my throat. "No, I've never asked someone to tell my fortune before."

She cocked her head, studying me. The flush faded from her face and her dark eyes sparkled. "Fortune telling?"

"Isn't that what the cards are for? Telling me what the future holds?"

"Not exactly, Rhys," she responded. "I do talk about the future with my clients, but there's more to it than that."

Her features had become more animated and bright. I wanted her to continue so I could keep that expression on her face. "Tell me more." Savannah hesitated, as though she wasn't sure of my sincerity. "I want to understand," I insisted.

"What I do isn't about telling the future or telling people what they should be doing. It's about introspection and intention. Tarot isn't some all-knowing set of cards. Each spread is meant to give you insight into your intention or question. The cards help you focus your energy and your thoughts in different directions or maybe help you find a different perspective."

Her explanation was interesting and captured my attention because it wasn't what I expected. "Will you show me?"

She smiled at me then, a wide, happy grin that lit up her face. "Of course. Let's do a reading." Savannah tilted her head and studied me. "I'll keep it simple. Three cards."

I watched as her nimble fingers shuffled the deck. She cut it several times then fanned the cards out in front of me. "Pick three cards. As you do so, think of your past, present, and future."

I hesitated. "I thought that readers didn't allow anyone to touch their cards? That is was bad luck or something."

"There are some that do feel that way," Savannah replied with a small smile. "I find that I prefer it, but I know others that don't like the energy left behind from querents touching their deck."

"Querents?"

Her smile widened. "The person seeking answers."

I nodded and studied the cards in front of me. "Three together or separately?" I asked, unsure of what she wanted of me. My past stretched so far behind me that there were times I could barely remember.

"Your choice," she stated with a small shrug. "Whichever cards grab your attention first, whether it's three all together or apart."

I looked at the line of cards in front of me, thought of my past, and touched the first card that caught my attention. I paused and lifted my eyes to Savannah. "What now?"

She reached forward and took the card, placing it face down in front of her. "Choose two more. Think of your present for the second and your future for the third."

I selected two more cards by touching them and she laid them next to the first. When I was done, she gathered the rest of the cards, stacked them, and set them to the side.

"A three card spread can represent many things. The past, present, and future, as we're doing right now. Or body, mind, and spirit. A particular situation, action you wish to take, and potential outcome. There are several other ways to apply a three card spread, but those are the three I use most commonly."

She enthralled me as she spoke. It wasn't just her words, but the way her aura pulsed with white light and color from her excitement and love of the subject. Her conviction and her enthusiasm were visible in the prism of light and color that shrouded her.

"Again, none of what we're doing here is to tell you what to do, only to make you think about what you've done in the past, what you're doing now, and give you something to think about when you deal with the future."

I nodded and watched as she flipped over the first card, revealing a heart pierced by three swords.

"This card represents your past," she began. "It's the three of swords, upright."

"But it's upside down to me, right?"

The corner of her mouth lifted. "Yes, but I usually read the cards facing toward me since I'm acting as the interpreter. Some readers do things differently, but this is what feels right to me."

I nodded, but my curiosity wasn't assuaged. "So the cards have different meanings based on whether their upright or not?"

Savannah leaned forward slightly, another small smile playing on her lips. "Every reader does it differently. Some don't consider their position, merely the overall meaning of the card. I prefer to think of them as upright or reversed because it does change the meaning somewhat. Now, the three of swords in this position usually represents some kind of loss or separation. A severing of ties or suffering. There's a lot of emotional conflict associated with this particular card. Maybe disputes with your family or friends." She glanced up at me and her face softened. "But all the pain is often followed by an opportunity for something new. A fresh start."

"And if it were reversed?" I asked.

"Then that would suggest you weren't learning or growing from the pain you endured. That you're stuck because you're hanging on to a grudge. It's similar to the upright, but there are small differences. The reversed indicates that you're approaching a situation with a closed mind rather than a willingness to learn."

I thought about everything that had happened in the last centuries. About Gaius, my master and then maker. About my brother, Cornelius, and his black soul. Suffering. A single word would never be enough to explain everything I'd experienced at the hands of Gaius and Cornelius. But I wasn't sure I would ever be able to let go of the past as Savannah suggested.

She seemed to be waiting for some sort of response from me, so I forced myself to nod my head. I wasn't willing to bare my soul to someone with so much beauty within her own. She didn't move to the next card right away, her eyes focused on me with an intensity that was nearly uncomfortable, as though she sensed the direction of my thoughts and didn't approve.

Finally, she flipped over the next card. "Temperance, upright," she stated. "This card in the spread represents your present. In the upright position, it means that you're trying to find a balance, reconcile two opposing sides of yourself. You feel pulled in different directions, but you'll be able to bring them together. It will be difficult, but if you persevere, you'll achieve something greater. You'll be stronger. The two halves of yourself will blend to make you better."

Her words struck a chord within me, resonating in my heart. Since my maker had taken part of my humanity from me, I'd often wondered if I was more a monster or man. But I seriously doubted I would ever be able to bring together those two sides of myself. Even if I wanted to, which I wouldn't. I didn't want to be a monster, even if it was only half of me.

Savannah's soft voice pierced my thoughts. "Are you okay, Rhys?"

I blinked and cleared my throat. "Yes, I'm fine. Please continue."

"Are you sure?" she asked. "You're welcome to discuss anything bothering you."

I lifted my eyes to hers. "I'm sure."

Her dark eyes were gentle as they moved over me and I could feel her compassionate heart reaching out to me. It took everything I had not to take what she offered so selflessly and without thought. But she didn't even realize I *could* take that from her. If she did, I knew she wouldn't be looking at me the way she was right now. There would be no softness in her gaze, no sweetness. Only fear and disgust.

"Let's just do the last card," I insisted, my voice rough.

She didn't argue, but I knew she was fighting the urge.

"The third card represents your future," she explained as she turned over the last card. "The Moon," she murmured. "That's strange. It's upright also. I haven't done a reading in a long time that had all three cards upright." She fell silent, staring at the card with concern on her face.

"What does it mean?" I prompted her.

"The Moon has many meanings," she began. "It can be a sign that things will be elusive, confusing, or in a state of flux in your life. The moon has a dark side, the side that remains unseen, which can symbolize that there are unknown forces or influences at work. But the moon also has phases and cycles, so it's important to think carefully before you take action because the next phase could be coming and your behavior could be detrimental rather than helpful. Since this last card represents your future, I would suggest that you verify facts and take a lot of time to consider the possible consequences for your actions." Her gaze rose to my face. "It's a mysterious card, one with many meanings but also many possibilities."

A chill of foreboding crept up my spine. Somehow the card felt like a threat or a warning. But a warning of what? I thought of the dreams I'd been having recently, only I wasn't so sure they weren't actually memories. If they were memories, they were Cornelius' and not my own.

"Rhys."

The sound of Savannah's voice brought my attention back to her. "Yes?"

Our eyes met. "If you need to talk about anything, I'm here. Whatever you say will stay between us. I don't want to overstep myself with you, but I'm concerned."

She meant every word that she said and I found that comforting. But I wouldn't do that. I'd learned long ago not to trust anyone with my problems. It was much safer for both of us.

"Thank you for the offer but I'm fine," I reassured her.

The open expression on her face slowly shut down and I could practically see the defensive wall she put up between us. "Okay then. Do you have any more questions about the tarot or the three cards?"

I regretted my words as soon as I heard the cool tone of her voice and the compassion that she offered me was retracted. I found myself saying something without thinking much about it. Since my conversation with Ava a few minutes before, I'd been considering her suggestion of purchasing a car to help me blend in. Then I made a split second decision. I wanted to spend more time with Savannah. "No, but there is one thing you can help me with."

Surprise radiated from her. "Of course."

"Do you know where I could buy a car?"

CHAPTER SIX

Savannah

A S I STOOD in front of my closet in my underwear, I put my hands on my hips and swore beneath my breath.

"How in the heck did I get myself in this darn mess?"

Okay, so I couldn't bring myself to swear, even though I wanted to. My grandmother hated curse words with a passion and always threw a fit whenever she heard me cuss. Now that she was gone, I found I still adhered to the habit she ingrained in me out of love for her and her memory.

Satchel mewed from the bed and I looked at her over my shoulder. The look she gave me conveyed her considerable boredom with this process. Rhys was meeting me in half an hour and I still had to put on make-up. When he'd asked me to help him with something a couple of days ago, my heart did a strange twist-leap in my chest. For some crazy reason, I'd automatically wondered if he was going to ask me out.

Silly me.

Instead, he'd asked me if I knew a good place to buy a car. To my surprise, he didn't have a vehicle. I agreed to drive him around to a few dealerships on my next day off, which was today.

"What is Mommy supposed to wear to shop for a car with her stupid hot neighbor, Satchel?" I asked her.

Her only reply was to turn her back on me and start licking her paw.

"Thank you. You've been very helpful."

With a sigh, I decided to ignore my cat and try to focus on my outfit. The weather was beautiful, warm and sunny. It was a gorgeous spring day, the kind of day that made me want to wear one of my maxi dresses with small straps and bright colors. But this also wasn't a date and I didn't want Rhys to think that I thought it was. Wow, that was a mouthful. Or a brain full since my entire conversation was in my head.

"God, now I'm confusing myself," I mumbled. Annoyed with my own wishy-washy behavior, I reached into the closet and grabbed the first dress I saw. I would wear what I usually wore. Would he even notice what I was wearing unless it was aggressively sexy? The thought made me laugh. Nothing I owned could be classified as aggressively sexy. Or even sexy at all.

The purple dress in my hand had a halter neckline with slender straps. The dress had a high waist and fell in voluminous folds to my ankles. I loved it because the color flattered my pale skin and dark hair and it was one of the most comfortable outfits I owned.

I slipped into the dress and slid my feet into flat tan sandals. A quick look at the clock made me wince. I didn't know Rhys very well, but he struck me as the kind of person who would show up five minutes early.

I hurried into my bathroom to finish getting ready. I pulled the sides of my hair back and pinned it in place with bobby pins. Then I put on a light layer of make-up. I brushed a little lavender shadow on my eyelids, applied mascara, and put a tinted balm on my lips. I had no sooner finished the final swipe before the doorbell rang.

"I knew he'd be early," I muttered to Satchel.

My cat followed me down the hall to the front door and sat on her rump, staring intently at the front door.

Pointing a finger at her, I admonished, "Don't even think about it. No clawing or biting my sexy neighbor. I want him to stick around for a few minutes."

Her imperious look told me to mind my own business.

"I mean it, Satchel," I said, pointing my finger at her.

She yawned.

"Dissed by my own cat," I grumbled. Taking a deep breath, I steeled myself before opening the door. It might have been crazy, but I felt like I needed a moment to prepare before I looked at him. If I took the time to ready myself, maybe I'd be able to string three words together without embarrassing myself.

I opened the door and immediately realized that I was wrong. Any words I planned to use vanished from my mind. Rhys stood on the porch wearing jeans, a t-shirt that hugged his upper body, and a pair of dark sunglasses. His dark blond hair was messy, as though he'd been running his hands through it, and his goatee looked fuller as though it needed a trim.

My brain cells didn't scream as they died, they swooned. The light spring breeze carried his scent into the house and my legs suddenly felt weak.

After we stood there staring at each other for a long moment, Satchel meowed. I jumped and gave myself a mental slap. "Hi, Rhys. Why don't you come in for a minute while I get my bag?"

I stepped back from the door to let him in and gripped the knob tighter as he passed me, his arm brushing mine. I had to get over my body's crazy reaction to his proximity. This was ridiculous and worse than any crush I'd had in middle school.

He stopped next to my cat, looking down at her. I couldn't read his expression because of the sunglasses he wore, but I could feel the slight buzz of his emotions, mainly curiosity and amusement. It seemed that with each of our interactions, small hints of what he was feeling would seep through the barrier that surrounded him.

"Who is this?" he asked, his mouth curving up slightly.

Surprised by his smile, I forgot my awkwardness. "That's my cat, Satchel."

His smile widened, nearly blinding me with its beauty. "Satchel? Like a bag? How did she get that name?"

"Uh, I found her, um, when she was a kitten and brought her home. She fit in my bag, so I, uh, named her Satchel." God, his smile should absolutely be illegal. Then I realized what he said. "Wait, how did you know she was a female?"

He chuckled. "She holds herself like a queen."

I sensed there was more to it than that, but I didn't press. "Well, let me go grab my stuff and we can head out. Do you want something to drink or anything while you wait?"

He shook his head, his face still downturned toward my cat. "No, thanks."

I walked out of the living room and into the kitchen, where my bag hung on a hook. I took a moment to make sure all the lights were off and Satchel had plenty of food and water before I went back into the living room.

When I entered, I stopped dead. Rhys was seated on the sofa with Satchel lying across his chest. While my cat wasn't mean or violent, she was aloof toward new people. Especially men.

Rather than ignoring Rhys as she usually did when a new person came to the house, she was cuddled up to him, her head tucked against his chin, purring so loudly I could hear her from several feet away.

"Your cat is very friendly," Rhys said, running his large palm over her back.

"Apparently, she is," I replied dryly.

"Are you ready?"

I nodded.

With one more stroke down Satchel's back, he gently set her to the side. "Bye, Satchel," he murmured.

Despite my attempts to remain strong, I melted at his farewell to my pet. Satchel shot me an annoyed look when we headed out the front door, letting me know that there would be retribution for me taking her new friend away.

When we climbed into my car I had to bite back a laugh when I saw that his legs were folded up nearly double. He seemed completely clueless on how to fix the issue so I pointed at the base of the seat. "Just reach underneath and pull the metal lever then slide the seat back."

He figured it out quickly, but didn't buckle his seatbelt after I started the car.

"Be sure to buckle up," I stated.

Rhys smiled, small but amused. "Why? I'm basically indestructible."

"Yeah, but I don't want to pay a fine if we get pulled over."

His smile widened, revealing long creases in his cheeks. Vaguely I wondered if they would be considered dimples but decided I didn't care because they were attractive regardless. "I'll pay the fine," he replied.

"Yeah, but it'll be on my record," I retorted.

Though he didn't say anything, his grin didn't fade and he reached for his seatbelt without further argument.

"Thank you," I murmured, putting the car in reverse and backing out of the driveway. "So, you weren't specific when you said you wanted to look for a vehicle. Did you decide if you want a car or a truck? Or maybe an SUV?"

"I think I'd like something larger than this. But I have no idea what you mean by SUV."

"Sports Utility Vehicle," I explained, struggling to keep my expression neutral. Ava said that Rhys was different and probably older, even centuries older, but he seemed somewhat ignorant of modern technology.

"What's that?"

I tried to think of the best way to explain it. "It's a cross between a car and a truck, but the rear area isn't open. The roof extends over the cargo space and there is a door in the back instead of a tailgate." I knew I wasn't using the correct terminology, but it was the best I could do.

"That sounds more like what I would want," he stated. "I don't care for trucks and most cars are too small for me."

"Okay, do you have any idea what make and model you want?"

His look said it all. I bit back a sigh. This excursion would likely extend into several days rather than one. I despised shopping for cars and only did it when I'd driven my previous vehicle into the ground. My current car was nearly a decade old and I intended to keep it for a couple more years if I could. I hated all the people and the smugness that rolled off the sales person when we finally agreed on a price. A price that was more than I should be paying.

"Well, the closest dealership sells Nissans. We could go check them out first."

"Let's do that," he agreed.

FIVE HOURS LATER, I was a bit shell-shocked. Rhys surprised me when we pulled into the Nissan dealership. Since I knew he would want a larger SUV, I parked near a group of Armadas. Within ten minutes, a man came out of the building behind the lot and introduced himself as Chris. I watched with concern as Rhys walked up to the white Armada with all the bells and whistles. Chris looked as though he wanted to turn cartwheels as Rhys circled the vehicle. I could feel the glee radiating from his body.

As they talked, I sidled toward the window and took a peek at the sticker. When I saw the asking price, my eyes nearly popped out of my head. He was looking at an SUV that cost more than my last three vehicles combined. Chris headed back into the building to get the keys and I stepped up next to Rhys.

"This is probably the most expensive SUV on the lot," I murmured.

Rhys looked down at me and smiled. "You think so?"

He seemed completely unconcerned and, considering he lived in a tiny rental home, I worried that he wouldn't have the funds for a vehicle like this.

"And the sales guy is practically salivating at the idea of you buying it."

"I know," Rhys replied, his grin growing wider. When he saw the worry on my face, he tilted his head. "I'll make sure he gives me a good deal."

Considering he'd told me that he'd never bought a car before, his words did nothing to soothe my concern. I had enough experience to know that haggling over a sticker price rarely ended up well for the buyer. "Okay," I said reluctantly. I decided to wait and watch.

The test drive was hair-raising, to say the least. Rhys seemed determined to test the vehicle's ability to handle turns at top speed. At one point I thought the SUV was up on two wheels. To my shock, Chris didn't say a word, though I did spot a few beads of sweat along his hairline. As Rhys made his way back to the dealership, he wove in and out of traffic so quickly that my stomach felt as though it were about to flop out of my body. I bit my bottom lip hard to keep myself from screaming in panic. I nearly sobbed in relief when I saw the dealership a block away and my heart was still pounding when we returned to the lot. Negotiations began in earnest then. The longer I watched Chris and Rhys interact, the more suspicious I became.

There was something slightly off about Rhys. I'd been so distracted by his blinding good looks before, but now that I wasn't the focus of his complete attention, I was beginning to notice things about him.

When Chris spoke, he listened intently, which I'd come to expect. However, even after the salesman stopped speaking, Rhys still seemed to be listening to something. He was also very in tune with what Chris was thinking and feeling. The longer I watched him, the clearer it became.

Rhys was some sort of telepath. I wasn't sure if he could read thoughts or emotions, but I knew he saw beyond the surface.

At the realization, I had to fight the urge to curl up into a ball in the corner or maybe find another place to live. It was highly likely that he knew how attractive I found him. He had to. My private feelings were out there, whether I liked it or not.

I was in a daze for the rest of the process, barely paying attention as Rhys negotiated with Chris over the purchase price.

Now, he was following me back to our street and I had no idea what to do. I felt as though my trust had been betrayed. But I also understood why he would keep it to himself. Even among the supernatural community, telepaths and empaths were considered outsiders and avoided. It was dangerous for anyone to know our secrets or to understand our innermost thoughts.

I should know. I'd been on the receiving end of suspicion and even disgust.

As I pulled into the driveway, I was struck with an epiphany. If I began avoiding Rhys because of his abilities, I was no different than the witches, vampires, and shifters that shunned me. He didn't ask for his gifts, and if he was anything like me, he probably thought of them as a burden.

I didn't want to be that kind of person. I wanted to be the kind of person I often wished to meet. Kind, compassionate, and accepting. Even with my abilities, I did the best I could to avoid invading someone's privacy. I didn't know Rhys very well, but he struck me as that type of person as well.

I needed to give Rhys a chance to do the same.

When I pulled into my driveway and parked, I got out of my car and watched Rhys turn his new SUV into his own drive. He climbed out and walked across the street toward me. My heart beat a little faster in my chest as I watched him. His walk was smooth and loose, as though he were in complete control of his body and he knew exactly what it was capable of. The underlying confidence in his every move was sexy.

He smiled as he approached me. "Thanks again for helping me today. I didn't realize driving a car was so much fun."

I found myself returning his smile. He sounded so sincere and serious. "It wasn't a problem. Honestly, I've never been on such a short car shopping trip. Usually it turns into an all day event." Then I comprehended exactly what he said. "You didn't realize driving a car was so much fun? Haven't you driven before? How did you talk them into letting you drive without a license?" I asked, my eyes wide.

Rhys laughed. "I recently learned an expression. *Money talks.* When Chris found out I was planning to pay cash today, he was willing to…overlook a few things."

"Oh my God," I gasped. Well, that certainly explained the test drive and the fact that I'd been strongly tempted to throw myself out of the SUV every time we stopped at a red light. I had to bite back the urge to recommend that he practice his driving skills. Or take a driving class.

He continued to chuckle. "I've ridden enough to learn a few things. But I'm glad you came with me today."

"I am too," I replied. I was also glad he hadn't gotten into an accident. He might be indestructible, but I certainly wasn't.

"I appreciate it. I've never—" He stopped speaking before he finished his thought.

I understood then that Ava had been right. It was unlikely Rhys knew anyone well enough to call them a friend. I might spend a majority of my time alone, but I did have friends and family. I had people in my life that cared about me and were willing to do things for me. Somehow I got the impression that Rhys did not. I didn't need empathic abilities to see that Rhys wasn't used to people helping him.

"It was fun," I said. It was a semi-lie. I enjoyed watching Rhys negotiate with the salesman and watching how animated he became when he haggled. The test drive and the process of buying the car, not so much.

He grinned. "You don't have to lie."

I recognized the teasing glint in his eyes and shot him a narrowed look. "Are you telepathic?"

Rhys shrugged. "Not exactly."

"Where exactly do your talents lie?" I asked.

I watched as the smile melted off his face and felt a pang of guilt. I hadn't meant to upset him, but his face revealed that I had. "I don't think I want to tell you," he replied.

Unable to stop myself, I reached out and touched his arm. I wasn't prepared for the sharp buzz of awareness that shot through my body, nor the subtle swell of his emotions. When I touched him, I had a stronger sense of what he was feeling. He was still muted and difficult to read but it was no longer impossible to discern his emotions. "Why not?"

His eyes locked on my fingers as they rested against his skin. "You won't want to talk to me anymore."

His honesty surprised me and left me breathless, like a blow to my belly. "Rhys," I whispered.

His gaze lifted to mine and I saw the pain there. I wasn't used to this. The barrier between us meant that I couldn't rely on the usual emotional cues to help me navigate our conversation. Instead, I was going on instinct.

"I'm not a good creature, Savannah," he declared quietly. "I've done things. Hurt people."

It was clear that it haunted him. I could feel the faint echoes of guilt and sadness resonate within him. Without thinking, I slid my hand down his forearm and laced our fingers together. "I don't believe you're a bad person, Rhys," I replied. Tension wound tighter inside him, so I decided to shift the topic a bit. "Look, I'm starving. I usually eat lunch earlier than this. Do you want to order a pizza and hang out for a little while longer? You might be able to convince Satchel not to murder me in my sleep."

Some of the pain cleared from Rhys' expression and he hesitated for a long moment. Finally, he said, "I enjoy pizza."

"I'll even share my wine with you," I offered.

Finally, his lips curved in a barely there smile. "If you insist."

Satisfied that I had pulled him out of the dark place in his head, at least for the time being, I released his hand and gestured for him to follow me. "Let's go inside. It's hot out here and I'm starving."

CHAPTER SEVEN

Rhys

I WATCHED AS Savannah moved around her kitchen with her cell phone pressed to her ear. She seemed to float rather than walk, her steps light and quick. With her multi-colored aura pulsing around her like a halo, she looked like an ethereal being, as though she belonged in another plane of existence. In my long life, I'd never seen the Goddess, but there was something about Savannah that made me think of the deity.

Then there was the dress she wore. The purple fabric was opaque in the sunlight that poured in from the kitchen window. I could see the shadow of her legs beneath the skirt. The sight distracted me, bringing up thoughts I had no business entertaining.

I didn't listen as she ordered the pizza, instead focusing on the movement of her hair against her bare shoulders and the light flush of pink on her cheeks. I knew she was attracted to me and I felt the same, but I would never act upon it. She didn't understand what I truly was. It would be wrong for me to take advantage of that.

I remembered the moment in her driveway when her fingers clasped my hand and the soft skin of her palm rested against mine. She hadn't believed me when I told her I was evil. She didn't understand that I was dangerous.

I shouldn't even be near her, but I couldn't stay away. The light that emanated from her soul was warm and bright and it drew me in despite my attempts to resist.

"Pizza should be here soon," she said, setting her phone on the counter. She glanced at me. "Do you want some salad with it?"

"You eat salad with your pizza?" I asked.

Savannah laughed and I relished the sound. I liked her laughter. It was vibrant and warm, much like her. "Not usually," she answered.

"Then don't worry about the salad."

She shrugged. "Fine with me." She moved to the fridge. "Do you want wine, soda, water, or something else?"

"Soda is fine," I answered.

Savannah smiled and took a bottle of wine and a can of soda out of the fridge. "More for me."

After she poured the soda into a glass and added ice, she handed it to me. "Thanks. Do you want me to open the wine?" I offered.

She laughed again, her face and eyes lighting up. "Don't worry about it. It's a screw top." Then she twisted the cap off the bottle and poured a glass for herself.

A delicate tap on my calf drew my attention down. Savannah's small grey cat looked up at me with expectant blue eyes, her paw suspended in the air in front of her. Understanding what she wanted, I reached down and lifted her in my arms. I'd always enjoyed the company of animals. They were simple creatures that typically wanted nothing more than a meal or attention. I'd never considered getting a pet before because I was constantly looking over my shoulder. Perhaps in time I could change that.

"Hello, Satchel," I greeted the animal.

She curled up against my chest, a rumbling purr emanating from her small body. Savannah studied us while she leaned a hip against the counter and sipped her wine. "Why did you say you weren't a good…creature?" She hesitated. "Do you think you're a creature rather than a person?"

I stared down at the glass in front of me. I didn't want to discuss this but she deserved to know. "I am a creature, Savannah. I may have begun my life as a man, but what I am now…I was created. I'm not human any longer. I haven't been for a long time."

She stood completely still and kept her gaze locked on mine. "Then what are you?"

"It's complicated," I evaded.

She leaned forward. "Rhys, I'm not going to judge you for something you have no control over."

"I don't understand."

Savannah put aside her wineglass. "Did you ask your creator to make you what you are?" she asked.

My only response was to shake my head.

"Did you want him to do this to you?"

"Of course not," I answered.

"Then what you are now is not of your doing. You had no control over this and what kind of person would I be to judge you harshly for it? I was born an empath. Do you know what that means?"

I nodded, wondering why she was bringing this up.

"Did you know that other supernatural beings loathe empaths and telepaths because of what we can do?"

I hadn't known that, but I could understand it. Anyone who could see into your mind or heart was dangerous when your life was full of as many secrets as ours were.

"I won't look at you differently, Rhys."

I knew that wasn't true. She might believe she was telling the truth, but knowing what I was would change her view of me. I liked the way she looked at me, the way she felt about me. I didn't want to change it. But I had to. She should know.

"Have you ever heard of the *animavore?*" I asked.

She appeared confused for a moment. "Creatures who consumed the souls of others? They've been extinct for millennia, if they ever existed at all. They're part of the dark lore in our history."

"They existed," I stated. "But to my knowledge, I'm the only one left."

Savannah's reaction didn't surprise me. Her eyes widened and her face paled. However, I was taken aback by her words. "I'm so sorry, Rhys."

I expected her to recoil in disgust when she heard what I was, not express sympathy. "I'm a vampire, Savannah. A parasite. I feed off a person's emotions. Their soul."

Speculation entered her gaze. "Do you often kill the people you feed from?" she asked. Once again, she reminded me of the Goddess, but now it was because wisdom and power were evident in her eyes. She might be gentle and nurturing, but she was also capable of great feats and ferocity.

"No, I never kill." I paused. That wasn't entirely true. I had killed my brother, Cornelius. I'd had no other choice. For century after century, he hunted me and took everything he could from me until I realized that I had no other choice. If I didn't stop him, he would kill me, then he would go on to hurt thousands, maybe even millions, of innocent people. Even now, the knowledge that I'd taken my brother's life still weighed so heavily.

When we were younger, before Gaius purchased us at a slave market, Cornelius had been joyful and kind. Gaius' attentions eventually hardened him and evil tainted his soul. When the experiments began, my brother was already a completely different person than the boy I'd grown up with. After Gaius succeeded in creating us, Cornelius was no longer human. Until the night I killed him, I'd often wondered if he even had a soul of his own left.

It wasn't until I drained the life force from his body that I'd had my answer. Cornelius had a soul, but it was so dark and tortured that any shred of humanity within him was lost millennia ago.

"Then how do you feed?" she asked me, her voice gentle.

I stared blankly at her. "What do you mean?"

"You need a person's soul to survive. That should be lethal. How do you feed without killing?"

"I don't need their soul in its entirety. The human soul is made up of many things but it's their emotions that I siphon. Sometimes at the deepest level." She didn't speak, merely met my gaze levelly, so I continued. "I choose victims who are in pain. Those who are hurting so badly that they're irrevocably broken. I feed on their agony, their heartbreak."

Savannah nodded. "What happens to them when you're done?"

"What do you mean?" I asked.

"Are they still in pain? Can they function?"

I stared at her, uncomprehending why this was important. "I remove part of their pain when I feed from them. It's an unfortunate side effect."

Her smile was small and sad. "Maybe, but maybe not. Did you ever stop to think that you might be helping these people by lessening their suffering?"

"That doesn't matter," I argued. "I'm stealing from them. Who we are is determined by what we experience in life. Pleasure, pain, joy, sorrow. Without the full range of human emotion, people never reach their potential."

"That's a good point," Savannah agreed. "But you're talking about people who are in despair. They aren't suffering from a short-term pain that teaches them an important lesson. They're battling demons with their bare hands, and they're losing. By lessening their burden, you might be helping them."

Her reasoning echoed my own justifications too closely to convince me. It was an empty reason. An excuse to make my actions seem less loathsome.

"Whether I'm helping them or hurting them doesn't matter. I'm taking something that is not mine. Especially something so essential."

She nodded. "I can understand why that concerns you. We're taught not to steal and to treat others with kindness but—"

Before the conversation could continue further, the doorbell rang.

"There's the pizza," she said, tearing her gaze from mine and taking a step toward the living room.

I got to my feet and bent down to place Satchel on the floor. "I'll get it." As I walked out of the kitchen, I pulled my wallet out of my pocket.

"I'll grab the plates and meet you in the living room," she called behind me.

When I opened the front door, a man stood on the porch with two pizzas in his hands. He blanched when he saw me. "Uh, hey. How are you today?"

"I'm doing well," I replied, wondering why he seemed unsettled. "How are you?"

"Um, I'm good, man." He looked around me, digging in his pocket for a slip of paper and pen. "Is Van here? I need her to sign the receipt."

"Receipt?"

"Yeah, she paid with her credit card so she needs to sign the receipt."

Before I could turn to find her, Savannah's warmth hit my side. "Hey, Tanner. How are you today?" She reached out and took the slip of paper and pen from the younger man.

He grinned at her, his eyes wandering over her face and shoulders. "I'm better now that I've seen you."

Savannah scoffed then laughed lightly. "Yeah, yeah. Stop flirting with me. I've told you more than once I'm too old for you."

"It's only five years," he argued.

"It might as well be fifty," she shot back.

He laughed, his eyes flicking to me for a moment, before he looked back at her. Something dark rose within me, a feeling I wasn't familiar with. I didn't like the way he looked at her and flirted with her right in front of me. It made me angry.

I stuck my wallet back in my pocket and reached out to take the pizzas from him as Savannah signed the paper. "I'll carry these into the living room," I stated.

Satchel appeared between Savannah and I and sat down on the floor. She looked up at Tanner with suspicious eyes. When he glanced down toward her, she growled at him. I could sense that she didn't like him either.

As I carried the pizzas to the coffee table, the cat followed me and I murmured to her, "Good girl."

Her only reply was to rub against my calf.

I set the pizzas down and stood next to the couch, watching as Savannah gave the receipt back to Tanner and brushed off his attempts at further flirtation.

"Go back to work," she admonished. "Flirt with someone your own age."

"But none of them are as pretty as you."

His reply had me biting back a growl of my own and tamping down on the urge to walk over and slam the door in his face.

"You're still getting the same twenty percent tip you always do," she retorted, putting a hand on her hip.

"I'll take a hug and a kiss instead," he offered.

Savannah laughed. "That hasn't worked the last ten times you've tried it and it's not going to work now. Thanks for the pizza."

Tanner chuckled as well. "It was worth a try," he sighed.

She shook her head. "Bye, Tanner."

"Bye, Savannah."

She didn't see it, but as she closed the door his eyes came to me. I saw and felt it clearly then. He was jealous. He wanted to be in my place. Then comprehension filled me. The dark feeling that I experienced earlier was also jealousy. Somehow, I'd formed an attachment to Savannah. I didn't want other men flirting with her or looking at her the way that Tanner did. I felt...possessive of her.

"I wanted to buy lunch," I commented as she sat on the couch and reached for the first box of pizza. "You helped me today."

Savannah waved a hand. "It was my pleasure."

"I still wanted to repay you."

She put two slices of pizza on each plate. "You can buy lunch next time then," she relented.

Pleased that she spoke as though she intended to spend time with me again, I let it go and sat down next to her.

"Want to watch TV or a movie?" she asked.

"Sure," I replied.

"What do you want to see?"

I shrugged and took a bite of my pizza. "I don't know. I don't have a TV."

Her eyes widened. "You don't have a TV?"

"No."

"I have no idea what to say to you now," she murmured.

"Why don't you show me your favorite television show?"

Her cheeks grew pink. "I don't know if you'd like it."

"I might not, but now I definitely want to see it because it's making you blush," I teased her.

Savannah laughed. "Fine, but no complaining if you don't."

I didn't tell her that I wouldn't complain even if I didn't because I wanted to learn more about her and understand who she was. The more I was around Savannah Baker, the more time I wanted to spend with her.

CHAPTER EIGHT

Savannah

TWO DAYS AFTER the car shopping expedition, Rhys texted me and asked me to help him buy a television. That particular shopping trip took longer than buying the SUV. In the end, he cooked dinner for us, which was a novelty I'd never experienced before. I enjoyed every minute of our time together and hope bloomed within me.

Then nothing. For over a week, I didn't hear from Rhys. He didn't call or text or even come into *The Magic Bean*. I never even saw a shadow in his window. Not that I took the time to look over at his house while hiding behind my curtains and blinds. That would be creepy. It was more of a casual glance from time to time. While standing behind my curtains. With all the lights off in the room. Okay, so maybe it was creepy. I was acting slightly stalker-ish.

I was beginning to wonder if the connection I felt with him was completely in my head. If the attraction that I thought he reciprocated was actually unrequited.

To combat my desire to brood, I dressed in a pair of ratty yoga pants and a ragged t-shirt and went out into my garden. Though both my front and back yards were small, I tried to make the most of them. When I started my garden, I wanted to create a whimsical fairyland and I thought I succeeded.

Lush plants and delicate flowers filled most of my front yard. A large oak tree soared over the house and cast shade across the lawn, which made it possible for me to plant flowers that grew best in the shade. Throughout the beds, I placed fantastical touches to bring fairytales and myths to life. Small stone fairies peeked around plants, wooden toadstools painted in bright colors were scattered strategically among the greenery, and other mythical creatures could be found nestled among the flowerbeds.

It took hours of work every week but I loved it. It was both relaxing and invigorating. I found that my mind was lighter after I spent a couple of hours in the garden and my body was pleasantly tired, making it easier to fall asleep after a stressful day.

Today, I decided to handle the weeding and removal of faded blooms from the plants. Settling into a rhythm that I found soothing, it was tedious work that would keep me occupied and prevent me from focusing too much on my thoughts.

Despite my confused feelings, I enjoyed spending time with Rhys. Because his emotions were so muted, I felt as though I could relax in his company. It was a strange sensation since I used so many emotional cues when I spent time with others. Instead I could focus on what he said and his actions rather than the ups and downs of his thoughts and feelings.

"Your garden is lovely."

I yelped and whirled around, falling onto my backside. A tall, slender woman with long black hair stood a few feet away. Even in dark jeans and a gauzy purple tank top, she was terrifyingly elegant. I could tell from a quick glance that her entire outfit was probably worth as much as my car. When my eyes landed on the bag dangling from her arm, I knew that the cost of the purse alone could have paid for a brand new sedan.

I rose to my feet, keeping my eyes on her. Despite her sophisticated appearance, something about this woman made the back of my neck tingle in a way I didn't like. Yet all I could sense emanating from her was general interest, nothing more. "Thank you. Can I help you?"

She walked toward me, her strides graceful and smooth despite the tall wedge sandals on her feet. She also managed to evade all of my flowerbeds with absolute grace. "Hi, my name is Rhiannon Temple. I'm a property developer and real estate agent. I'm interested in this area. Have you ever considered selling your home?"

As she spoke, she removed a business card from her bag. When she held it out to me, I took it automatically.

"Unfortunately, I rent this home," I replied. A slightly painful shock jumped from her fingers to mine for the brief moment that we held the card between us, then she released it and the sensation faded. "But you can speak to my landlord. Her name is Ava Amaris and she owns *The Magic Bean* coffee shop on South Congress."

Rhiannon nodded her head, her black hair falling like in a sleek sheet down her back. "Thank you. I appreciate the information." Her eyes wandered over the plants in my garden. "You've made this place beautiful."

"Thank you." Courtesy dictated I invite her inside and maybe offer her something to drink, but my instincts were shrieking at me to keep her out of my home.

I was saved from having to make an excuse by the sound of Rhys' voice.

"Savannah, I'm glad I caught you at home. Do you have a minute?"

Rhiannon and I turned toward him.

"Sure, Rhys," I replied. I glanced at Rhiannon. "I'll let Ava know you came by but if you'd like to speak with her in person, she'll be in the shop next week."

I tried to ignore the way that Rhiannon eyed him because I disliked the feeling it stirred within me. Jealousy. Plain and simple. I wanted to smack her as she longingly ogled Rhys from head to toe. He was *my* stupid hot neighbor. Mine.

"Hello," she greeted him, holding out her hand. "I'm Rhiannon Temple."

Rhys took her hand, but released it quickly. "Good afternoon."

When he didn't say anything else, the woman seemed undeterred. She reached back into her bag, coming out with another card. "I'm a property developer and real estate agent and I'm interested in homes in this area—"

Rhys lifted a hand. "Thank you, but I rent my home from the same landlord as Savannah. You'll have to speak to her."

With a polite nod, Rhiannon returned the card to her purse. "Thank you for the information." She encompassed us both with a look. "I appreciate your time. Have a lovely afternoon."

Rhys and I watched as she strode gracefully down the sidewalk and climbed into a white Range Rover that was parked several houses down.

It wasn't until she drove away that he turned to me. "Are you okay?"

I blinked at him in confusion. "Yes, of course. Why wouldn't I be?"

He tucked his hands into the pockets of his jeans and rocked back on his heels. "You seemed uncomfortable when you were speaking to her."

I couldn't deny it, so I shrugged and looked down at the toes of my dirty sneakers. "There was something unsettling about her, that's all. But thank you."

"You're welcome."

We stood in my front yard in silence for a long moment. "Your garden truly is beautiful," he said. After he spoke, a light breeze picked up and made the wooden and metal wind chimes hanging from the oak tree sing. "It's almost as if it belongs in a different world."

"Thank you. That's exactly what I want it to be."

Once again neither of us said anything else for a few seconds. Just when I was about to excuse myself and hide inside, he focused his eyes on me. The color startled me for a moment. They were brilliantly blue and piercing, as though he could see into my soul. Which he technically could, I realized.

"Would you go somewhere with me this afternoon?" he asked.

Unable to resist, I teased, "Do you need help buying a refrigerator or a laptop?"

Rhys smiled. "No, I discovered a beautiful place and I think you would enjoy it."

Seeing the dimples in his cheeks, I couldn't say no, even though I was still a little upset I hadn't heard from him in a week.

"Let me go change."

CHAPTER NINE

Rhys

I HAD NO idea what I was doing as I steered the SUV into the parking lot at Zilker Park. The botanical gardens were beautiful. I discovered them my second week in Austin and came here regularly. So regularly that the attendant, Joe, greeted me by name when I pulled up to pay the entry fee.

Savannah was watching me with open curiosity as I parked. "Do you come here often?" she asked.

I shrugged. "Once or twice a week."

She looked around. "What is this place? I've lived in Austin for years and I've never been here."

"It's a botanical garden."

"It's so pretty," she murmured.

As we got out of the car, I noted that clouds were gathering in the sky. I hoped the rain would hold off for a bit so I could show her my favorite spot. I wanted to reach for her hand, but I suppressed the urge. I should be keeping my distance from her, not trying to pull her closer. I shouldn't have even brought her here, but once I spoke to her again and saw the gentle warmth in her dark eyes, I found myself inviting her to join me.

First, we walked through the Butterfly Garden, admiring the flowers and the beautiful wings of the butterflies that skimmed from bloom to bloom. Then I led her to my favorite area in the garden. Lush green trees and grasses lined the stone path that led to the koi pond.

Savannah sighed when she saw it. "This is so peaceful," she murmured. "And beautiful."

I knew she would see it as I did. Beauty and peace in a busy world. A place to breathe.

"I try to find peace where I can," I replied. "There is so little of it in this world."

Her head turned toward me. "I don't agree with that."

Surprised, I met her gaze. "You don't agree?" I asked in confusion.

"That there's very little peace in this world," she clarified. "I think there is plenty of peace, even in the middle of a busy city. You just have to be willing to experience it."

"How do you mean?" I asked. Savannah often said and did things that made me wonder how she saw the world. Her perception was so different than mine.

"Peace isn't always found. Sometimes, we have to make our own."

"That doesn't make sense," I disagreed.

She laughed and shook her head. "Don't be so literal, Rhys. It's possible to be peaceful in the midst of chaos. You only have to look for your opportunity. Like my garden. We live in a crowded area. Lots of homes and people everywhere. Yet I feel my calmest when I'm working there. I find serenity there because that's where I want to find it. That's where I look for it."

Strangely, her reasoning made a great deal of sense. I'd never looked for tranquility wherever I could find it because, until Cornelius died, I hadn't believed it existed. I was still learning how to relax, but I doubted I would ever stop looking over my shoulder.

Savannah returned to her contemplation of the koi pond. "Can I ask you something?"

Unsure of why she was requesting permission to ask me a question, I replied, "Of course."

"How old are you? You look around my age, maybe in your late twenties, but your accent and the way you speak…" She fell silent.

I knew that I sounded antiquated when I spoke because I rarely spent time with other people. I also knew I needed to work on that in order to assimilate into modern society, but I loathed the idea of spending so much time around other people. Crowds made me feel under attack.

"The answer to that question is complicated," I replied.

"You don't have to tell me if—"

"It's not that I don't want to tell you," I interrupted. "I'm not sure if I can."

She looked up at me, a frown tugging at her brow. "What do you mean?"

"When I was born, record keeping was not as important as growing enough food to survive in my village. My first master said I was born in the spring and I do know that was about a century before what you call the Common Era."

Her eyes widened. "You were born *before* the Common Era? That means you're over two thousand years old."

"I feel every single year," I sighed.

"Now I really have a ton of questions," she said, her voice high. Savannah took a deep breath and studied my face. "But they can wait. This place is where you come to relax."

My body stilled completely as she faced the koi pond again and slid her palm into mine. The contact was unexpected, but sweet. Reflexively, my fingers tightened around her hand. Our arms brushed with each breath, making me aware of her body in a way I was unable to ignore.

We stood there in silence until a crack of thunder interrupted the tranquility. A few seconds later, the skies opened up and released sheets of rain. She yelped, instinctively lifting her arm above her head as though it would protect her. Quickly, I decided our best course of action was to head up to the teahouse perched on top of the hill behind us. I helped Savannah up the stone steps toward the top of the garden where the teahouse sat overlooking the greenery and had a view of downtown Austin.

Holding hands, we dashed under the cover of the teahouse. Savannah looked up at me as she laughed and drops of water sparkled on her face. Joy radiated from her face and it was so pure and sweet, I couldn't resist her any longer. It might be a mistake that I'd regret later, but I couldn't stop myself.

Holding both of her hands in mine, I leaned down and pressed my lips to hers. Savannah froze. Her body stiffened and her hands clamped down around my fingers, pressing our joined hands against my legs. I nearly pulled away, but she suddenly softened and I was no longer thinking about ending the kiss. She leaned into me, her breasts pressing against my torso, and I was surrounded by her scent intermingled with the smell of rain. It was an intoxicating combination. Her lips clung to mine as her hands crept up to my neck and wrapped around me.

The kiss was light, nearly chaste, but it still had the power to knock me on my ass. I could feel the hunger rising inside me, the urge to plunder, to take what I wanted. Savannah hummed against my lips, opening her mouth beneath mine, and I no longer thought of anything but tasting her.

The feelings I'd been suppressing over the last weeks exploded and I wrapped my arms around her waist, gathering her to my body. Savannah fisted her fingers in my hair, her fingernails scraping against my scalp. The hum in her throat became a moan and her body undulated against mine. My fingers dug into her hips, pressing her closer. The embrace was beyond my control and I couldn't stop, even if I wanted to.

Another rolling boom of thunder made her flinch and broke through the heated haze that surrounded my mind. We stood in the circle of each other's arms for a long moment, both of us breathing hard. Gradually, Savannah withdrew enough to look up at my face.

Her smile was tremulous, as though she could sense my doubts and fears. "It's been a long time since anyone's kissed me like that," she murmured. Her fingertips lifted to my lips, brushing lightly across them. "Well, actually, no one's ever kissed me like that."

The stab of guilt pierced my heart. I had no right to put my hands or my mouth on this warm, gentle creature. Despite her reassurances that she didn't think I was a monster, I knew better. This couldn't happen again. While I couldn't regret it, I also understood that I couldn't repeat it.

I released her slowly, making sure that she had her balance before I stepped back. "I'm sorry, Savannah."

She frowned at me. "Sorry? For kissing me?"

"I shouldn't have done that."

Savannah rocked back on her heels and stared at me, her dark eyes piercing in a way I'd never seen before. "I'm pretty sure it takes two to kiss."

"Savannah, I can't do this with you. It's wrong."

Her body grew rigid. "Wrong?" Her eyes moved to a point over my shoulder and I realized she misunderstood what I was trying to say.

"Savan—"

"You're right, Rhys. This would be wrong. I don't want to push you into something that you aren't interested in."

I nearly laughed at her words. If she hadn't felt my interest earlier when I kissed her, I wasn't going to point it out.

With her gaze returning to mine, Savannah continued, "I want the person I'm with to be one hundred percent sure that they want to be with me." She smiled, but for the first time since I met her, it didn't reach her eyes. "The rain has let up, so why don't we head back to the house?"

It seemed there was nothing else to say.

CHAPTER TEN

Savannah

MY ATTENTION WANDERED as I sprayed the table with disinfectant and wiped it down. Mechanically, I moved to the next table and repeated the process.

"Earth to Savannah," Ava called. "Come in, Savannah. This is your captain speaking."

I looked over at her and shook my head. "You realize that makes no sense, right?"

"Why not?" she asked as she mopped the floor.

"Because the captain would be on the space ship with me, not on Earth."

Ava laughed as she moved the bucket over and began cleaning another section of the floor. It was rare that she scheduled me to help close during the week, but Wednesdays the Bean closed down at six and we usually went out to dinner. Well, one of us picked up dinner on the way to my house. I rarely went to Ava's. She was always welcoming while I was there, but I got the impression that she didn't like people in her space. Also, Satchel loved Ava. Almost as much as she adored Rhys. Clearly, my cat was indiscriminate with her affections. Except with me. Most of the time, she barely tolerated me.

"I've been talking to you for the last five minutes," Ava teased.

"Where was your head?"

I shrugged and went back to wiping tables. "Nowhere."

Ava's eyes narrowed on me. "Not on your hot new boyfriend?"

The laugh that escaped me was bitter rather than amused. "What boyfriend?"

"Rhys!" she exclaimed. "As I recall, you two were spending a lot of time together a couple of weeks ago."

I shrugged and finished cleaning the last table. To keep myself busy, I carried the towel and cleaning solution behind the counter and put it away. "We spent two days together. That's it," I answered.

"Savannah Lydia Baker, look at me."

Recognizing that tone of voice as the same one my mother used when she knew I was evading her, I faced Ava.

"What happened?" she asked, propping herself up with the mop.

"He kissed me," I answered, trying not to think about that kiss. If I'd needed any proof that my attraction to him wasn't one-sided, that kiss had been it. My head had felt as though it were about to explode. Or maybe that was my underwear. Either way, something on my body had been perilously close to catching fire.

Ava's eyes rounded. "And that means he's *not* your boyfriend?" she asked.

"It is when he stops and tells you that it was a mistake. Then he finishes it up with how it would be *wrong*," I emphasized the word and made air quotes with my fingers, which made Ava roll her eyes. "To be with you. I don't want to be with a man who thinks it's wrong to be with me! There's nothing wrong with me. Much."

Ava scowled. "There's nothing wrong with you. Period. End of story." She paused and seemed to consider something for a moment. "But have you thought about the fact that maybe he thinks it's wrong because of who he is rather than who you are?"

"Huh?" I had no idea what she was trying to say.

Ava sighed and swiped the mop across the floor one last time before she put it in the wringer in the bucket and rolled it toward the back room. "What I mean is that Rhys strikes me as an old soul who's experienced a lot of pain. Maybe he thinks that he's taking advantage of you if he gets involved."

Since Rhys had said something about being a monster and a parasite before, her words definitely made sense. This was exactly why my interactions with him confused me so badly. With his muted emotions, I couldn't read Rhys clearly. It was easier if we were touching, but he was still somewhat blocked. After he kissed me at the botanical gardens, my own emotions had been in such a tailspin I'd been unable to read anything of his.

"Maybe," I replied. "But I'm not going to push it. I might be lonely and I might want someone to love me, but I'm not going to beg him for attention. If he wants me, he knows exactly where to find me."

"We should do a reading," Ava stated. "Just to get a sense of what's going on."

I shook my head. "Nope. Not gonna do it. I know exactly what's going on. Rhys is either too afraid to get involved with me or he truly believes he's not good enough for me. Either way, the only person who can change his mind is himself. I'll do a lot of things for love, but I won't do that."

"Did you just quote a song?" Ava asked.

I frowned at her. "Maybe, but not intentionally."

"Okay, so no tarot reading," she agreed. "How about Thai food, ice cream, and wine?"

"Add movies that make me laugh and you have a deal," I replied.

Ava smiled. "I can do that."

"Fine. My house or yours?"

"Yours," she said immediately. "I need cuddles from Satchel."

I rolled my eyes. "I think you've been replaced as her favorite person. Brace yourself."

"What? Not possible," Ava scoffed.

I nodded. "She loves Rhys. Sometimes she'll sit on the back of the couch and stare out the window at his house. If I try to talk to her, her tail twitches and she glares at me as though she's plotting my demise."

"Okay, so I'll stop and get her a little present on my way too. I don't want her to kill my favorite employee."

That wasn't saying much. She often hired college students to work part time throughout the year, but the turnover was high. She and I were the only tarot readers as well.

"Bribery might work," I agreed.

"Great. I'll meet you at the house in half an hour."

We decided that she would get the wine and ice cream and I would order the Thai before we parted ways. I walked home in the early evening light, calling the restaurant as I strolled down the sidewalk. The sun would be going down soon and the sunset promised to be spectacular. Maybe I could talk Ava into sitting in my back garden to drink our wine and eat our take-out. Despite my plans to pretend it didn't exist, I found myself glancing at Rhys' house. There was a single dim light on in the front window and I knew he was likely sitting in his living room, reading a book or watching television. I wondered how he had been since the last time I saw him, but I tried to shove him out of my head. He'd made a decision and I wasn't going to argue about it.

Maybe it was pride but I would not chase after a man, no matter how ridiculously hot he was. I might have strange talents but a man should want me enough to pursue me. Especially in the beginning.

Resolutely, I turned away from Rhys' house and moved up the

sidewalk toward my front door. Satchel sat on the windowsill, her little gray body wedged behind the blinds, and her blue-green eyes were full of accusation. When I opened the door, she ran over to me, meowing and blinking rapidly. I wasn't sure if she was telling me all about her day, giving me the rundown of Rhys' activities, or chewing me out for being gone until so late. However, when I leaned down to pet her, she reared back and pawed lightly at my hand until I picked her up and cuddled her to my chest.

"So you still love your mommy, I see," I murmured as I shut the front door behind me and went through the house, turning lights on. I went straight back to the bedroom and changed into yoga pants and a t-shirt, relishing in the comfort.

A few minutes later, there was a knock on the door and I knew it was Ava before I opened it because of Satchel's reaction. She ran straight for the door and stood on her back legs, batting at the wood with her front paws as she meowed loudly.

When I opened the door, Ava swept inside, holding four bags.

"How many bottles of wine did you buy?" I asked, taking two of the bags from her.

"Three."

"Ava! We barely finish two between us. Why do you always bring so much wine? I think I still have a bottle left from last time."

"That may be true, but our usual dinners are just for fun. This has to do with man trouble. Man trouble always equates to an extra bottle of wine."

"What's in the other two bags?"

"Four flavors of ice cream."

I let my head fall back and I addressed my ceiling. "She wants my ass to be wider than it already is."

"Whatever, you have a fantastic ass. Very J.Lo. Men love that."

"If you're going to say things like that, I definitely will need the third bottle of wine after all."

I put the ice cream in the freezer as Ava poured us each a glass of wine. As though it were choreographed, the doorbell rang, announcing the arrival of our dinner. I managed to talk Ava into eating dinner on my back deck and we enjoyed the changing colors of the sky while the sun went down.

The idyllic moment made me think of my conversation with Rhys at the botanical garden. Peace could be found in the least likely places if you just took a moment to look for it. This evening, this moment in time with my best friend, was the essence of tranquility.

"What are you thinking about?" Ava asked me.

I picked up my glass of wine and sipped before I answered her. "Rhys."

She pushed her empty plate aside and leaned back in her chair, swirling the wineglass in her hand as she regarded me intently. "Are you finally going to tell me what happened?"

I sighed and drained my glass. As I poured another, I answered, "You know, it's strange. I barely know him, yet I feel a connection to him that I've never felt with anyone else. Not even Neil."

Neil was my last boyfriend. We'd dated my junior year in college. He had been four years older than my twenty-one and a great deal more mature than the boys I went to school with. He was a wonderful man but we discovered after a few months together that we just didn't work. I was a homebody and, to an extent, he was as well, but he did like to go out and try new restaurants. I always found it difficult to frequent such public places because I was constantly bombarded with the emotions of the people around me. While most restaurants might seem like they were full of fun and happy people, nothing could have been further from the truth. Beneath the bright surface, I could feel the darkness of the thoughts that surrounded me. Pain, anger, disappointment, frustration, jealousy. Those emotions were almost painful when I was exposed to them for too long.

Neil wanted to have children, but I told him I wasn't sure. After the relationship ended, I realized my uncertainty had more to do with our relationship and not because I didn't want a child. I loved children. They broadcasted every emotion they felt at full volume, but there was no underlying agenda or malicious intent. While there was an exception to every rule, I found my interactions with children to be satisfying and fun.

Neil would make a wonderful partner for a lucky woman, but I was also relieved that lucky woman wasn't me.

"Wow, that's pretty serious," Ava replied, taking me away from my thoughts of the past.

"Yeah, it is," I answered, taking another sip of my wine. "At least on my part." I recognized that I was getting tipsy, but I didn't care. I needed to cut loose. I hadn't talked to Ava about Rhys since the kiss in the park because I wasn't sure how I felt about him. Now I knew.

Rhys could have been a man I fell hard for if he hadn't been too stupid or too scared to realize that we shared something special. It might have been in its infancy, but our connection had the potential to become my extraordinary ordinary.

"So, what now?"

"Nothing," I replied with a shrug. "He made his choice. I made mine. We're going our separate ways."

"Why do men always seem to have their heads up their asses? Do they like the view?" she asked, annoyance easily discernible in her tone.

I giggled. Then I snorted. My giggles became full-blown laughter. Ava joined me. "Like the view?" I questioned, snorting again. "I need to remember that. I'm going to have to use it."

"You don't curse, remember?" she pointed out.

"I might start just to tell that joke."

Ava shook her head. "It wasn't that funny, silly."

Maybe not, but I hadn't laughed much over the last few weeks. It was nice to let it out.

"Are you ready to eat ice cream straight from the carton and watch a funny movie?" she asked. "From what I understand, that's practically a requirement when you have man trouble."

"That's a cliché," I argued.

"Maybe, but it sounds like fun."

She had an excellent point. "Okay, but I want to try something. I found this recipe on that pinning website. You take ice cream or sherbet and pour sparkling wine over it."

Ava perked up in her seat. "So it's a dessert that will also make you tipsy? Count me in!"

We gathered our plates and went inside for the movie and dessert. As I poured more wine and dished up ice cream, I said to Ava, "You know, I feel like we're always talking about the state of my love life but you never bring up yours."

She glanced at me with a droll look. "That's because I don't have a love life."

"Why not?" I asked, genuinely curious. Despite our long friendship, Ava was an intensely private person. She rarely talked about her past or her relationships. I couldn't remember the last time she even mentioned going out on a date.

A wistful expression flitted across her face. She looked a little lost and wishful. "No one seems…right," she explained. "It's like a piece of me is missing. An empty space that's just for one person. Every time I meet a man, I feel as though I'm comparing him to someone else, even though there's never been anyone else. After a while, I just gave up. It's not fair to him if the relationship drags on and I'm not completely invested."

While I understood what she was saying, I could also feel the yearning within her for a partner. For love. "But if you don't look for your missing piece, how will you ever find it?"

Ava laughed, but there was very little humor in it. "It's been centuries, Savannah. I doubt I'll ever find what I'm looking for."

I swallowed hard at her statement. I had always sensed that Ava had lived a long time, but centuries seemed longer than I expected. If I were achingly lonely after twenty-eight years, how would I feel after hundreds?

Ava seemed to sense my sadness and she smiled at me. "I've been around for a very long time. I love my life and I'm accustomed to being alone. I'm not pining away for the love of my life."

"How old are you?" I asked her. "You've never answered me when I asked before, but now I really want to know."

"I'd say I'm a few years older than Rhys," she replied.

Though I suspected she was older than she appeared, I hadn't expected that answer. How was it I managed to befriend two supernatural beings that were both thousands of years old?

"You were not the only lonely person when we met, Savannah," she murmured. "And you were not the only one who needed saving." Before I could respond, she gathered her bowl of ice cream and glass of wine. "Now, enough of this depressing stuff. I came here to cheer you up, not make you feel worse. Let's go watch a movie, eat ice cream, and get tipsy."

Feeling as though my perception of Ava Amaris had just been changed forever, I picked up my own bowl and glass and followed her into the living room.

CHAPTER ELEVEN

Rhys

I STOOD IN front of my refrigerator with the door open and stared inside. I was uncertain what I wanted to eat and my stomach was growling angrily. Since the day I'd kissed Savannah in the garden, my appetite for food was unpredictable. I wouldn't feel like eating a single bite for days at a time, and then I was ravenous. I knew that I needed to eat, but everything tasted like dust. I hadn't gone to the grocery store in over a week and my pantry was very nearly bare.

I hadn't been sleeping well since that day either. My dreams were strange and frightening. A woman with long dark hair and black eyes haunted me. She looked exactly like Rhiannon Temple but she was dressed in clothing from centuries ago. After I absorbed Cornelius' power, I often had peculiar dreams and I realized I was experiencing his memories. I couldn't decide if the recent dreams I'd been having were Cornelius' memories with Rhiannon's face injected or my subconscious response of dealing with the suspicion she roused in me.

Then there was the kiss. As the weeks wore on, I began dreaming of Savannah more and more, reliving the moment of that kiss. Sometimes the memory would meld with the dream and I wouldn't stop kissing or touching her. Other times I had to experience the moment I told her it was a mistake over and over. The pain in her eyes and the way her expression shut down when I spoke made my chest ache. It wasn't surprising that my appetite was ruined.

The doorbell rang, saving me from searching for food that wasn't there. I shut the fridge with a sigh and walked to the front door. When I saw who stood outside, I was tempted to ignore her presence, but she was my landlord and I knew she had a key.

"Good evening, Ava," I greeted her when I opened the door.

She didn't reply as she walked past me into the house.

"Please, do come in," I commented dryly.

Ava turned on me. "What exactly are you doing with Savannah?" she asked.

I frowned at her, not sure I understood why she was here. "Nothing. I haven't spoken to Savannah in weeks."

"I know!" she exclaimed. "Why aren't you talking to her?"

My body tensed at her question. "I'm not sure how any of that is your business," I replied, my voice cold and harsh. "You're my landlord, not my friend."

She winced briefly and tried to hide it, but I saw it all the same. Still, her voice was gentler this time when she spoke. "Do you know why I offered you this house?"

I shook my head and shut the door I was still holding open.

She took a deep breath. "I saw in you what I see in Savannah. You're looking for your place in this world. But your place isn't in a particular city or country, it resides within another person." I shook my head in denial, but Ava just smiled and continued. "You're not the only one who can see into the heart of people, Rhys. As soon as I met you, I saw your deepest desire. You want someone to love who will love you in return. You want to go to sleep every night knowing that there is someone in this world who cares for you. And I can't blame you for that. It's one of the most basic human desires, the desire to be loved. Yet it's the most difficult to confess."

"But I'm not human," I argued.

Her expression grew alert at my words. "Out of everything I just said, it's interesting to me that you latched on to that particular statement. You won't deny your deepest desire, but you deny your humanity."

"I'm not human," I repeated. "I haven't been human since Gaius made me what I am."

Ava considered me, her gaze strangely intense. "Maybe not completely, but you're still mostly human. You may need something more than food and water to survive, but you're not a monster."

I didn't disagree with her aloud, but she seemed to read my thoughts clearly.

"That's why you stopped talking to Savannah, isn't it?" she asked. "Because you believe you're evil and you don't want to taint her."

I jerked my chin. "I think it's time for you to go."

Ava moved toward me, her eyes shifting and shimmering, becoming more blue than purple. I watched in awe as her face seemed to glow with an inner light. I realized it was her power. Ava Amaris held tremendous magic within her body, so much that it bled from her skin and eyes, lifting her hair with an invisible wind. How she leashed it, I couldn't understand. From this distance, I could feel the pulse and weight of it.

"Rhys of the Dark, you have never been a monster. I can see inside you. I know how you were made and what you carry within you. If you were what you believed yourself to be, I would never have allowed you into my shop, much less into my life. It is time for you to release the past and move toward the future." Even her voice resonated with magic.

I shook my head. "Stop it, Ava. You don't know what you're

talking about."

Slowly, the glow that emanated from her receded and there was one last pulse of her power before it withdrew. Once again, she was the small blonde woman with strange purple eyes. She appeared completely normal, as though the last few seconds had never happened.

"I do know," she replied in a whisper. "I know what it's like to walk around in your body, feeling as though what's inside you is dangerous. And it is, but you are what you are and you can choose how you wield your strength. Those choices are what make you a good man instead of a monster. I *know*, Rhys. You and I are more alike than you realize."

Her words were insidious, creeping inside me and creating cracks in the shield I'd created around my heart. Though I would never admit it, I wanted to believe her. I wanted to believe I could have someone like Savannah in my life. No, not someone like Savannah, but Savannah herself.

"If you give her a chance," Ava murmured. "Savannah will show you exactly how she sees you and you'll understand that she is right. She brings out the best in people because that's what she sees. If you give her time, you'll realize that she does the same for you."

I hesitated. Ava was telling me everything I wanted to hear and my own heart yearned for the picture she painted regardless of the possibility that I might hurt Savannah.

"Give yourself a chance, Rhys. And give her a chance. I've never seen her like this."

That got my attention. "Like what?"

Ava shook her head. "No, it's not my story to tell. I shouldn't have even mentioned it, but I can't stand to see her hurting."

I knew I'd hurt Savannah after I kissed her, but I thought she would recover quickly. We barely knew each other.

"Will you talk to her?" Ava asked.

I relented. "Yes, I'll talk to her."

Ava smiled brightly. "Great. Then you should put some shoes on."

"What? Why?" I asked, frowning at her.

"Because you're coming with me to Savannah's house for dinner. She's making my favorite—Salisbury steak and mashed potatoes."

"Ava, maybe—"

"Go put your shoes on and come with me," she commanded. Her tone brooked no argument.

Unaccustomed to someone telling me what to do, I balked.

"Rhys, this is your opportunity to get what you want and to give the same to Savannah. Take it or regret it for the rest of your extremely long life."

With that, she walked out the front door, shutting it softly behind her. Without thinking about what I was doing, I went into my bedroom and grabbed my sneakers. I tied them on quickly and left the house.

As soon as I knocked on Savannah's door, it opened to reveal Ava. "I knew you'd make the right choice." She turned away from me and called out. "We've got one more for dinner!"

"What?" Savannah asked, her voice floating out of the kitchen. "Who?"

Ava led me into the kitchen. "I invited Rhys. I thought he could use a good home-cooked meal."

As soon as I saw Savannah's face and her demeanor, I regretted what I had done weeks ago. The light I was so accustomed to seeing within her was snuffed. I felt like shit.

She was staring at me in surprise, the spoon in her hand poised over the pan on the stove.

"Hi, Savannah," I said.

When I spoke, she visibly gathered herself. "Hi, Rhys. How have you been?" Then she peered down into the pan in front of her, stirring the contents.

The stiff formality in her voice made me wince. And the fact that she wouldn't look at me? I hated it. I'd broken something between us when I kissed her and then turned away. I sensed it would take quite a bit of work to fix it.

I glanced at Ava, who nodded and left the room, and then stepped closer to Savannah. "Not so good," I replied.

Her head came up then and she peered at me. "What?"

I turned so that I faced her, keeping space between us, and leaned a hip against the counter. Crossing my arms over my chest, I answered, "You asked how I've been. I haven't been doing well."

Some of the blankness left her eyes as concern crept in. "What's wrong?"

This would be the difficult part. I wasn't accustomed to talking to other people, much less admitting my feelings. "I hurt you and, in the process, hurt myself."

Her brows drew together. "What do you mean?"

"I made a mistake at the park a few weeks ago."

She turned her face away from me then. "I know, you said as much then."

"That's not what I'm referring to," I stated. When she still wouldn't look at me, I continued, "I shouldn't have said that to you because it wasn't a mistake."

Savannah looked at me then. "It wasn't?"

"No, it's not something either of us should regret."

"Then what are you talking about?"

"I shouldn't have said what I did after," I admitted. "I shouldn't have hurt you."

"But if that's how you feel, you should be honest," Savannah replied, her face sad.

"Maybe, but I don't truly feel that way. I didn't want to push you away, but I felt I had to."

Her dark eyes moved over my face as though she were trying to get a sense of what I was feeling. Or if I was telling the truth. "Why did you think you had to push me away?"

"Because I didn't want to hurt you."

Savannah frowned in confusion. "So you hurt me in order not to hurt me?"

I ran a hand over my hair, feeling as though I were fucking this up somehow. "I didn't see it that way at the time. I thought..." I stopped speaking, unsure if I could admit what I was truly thinking.

"You thought what?"

"I didn't think it would truly hurt you. I wasn't sure you felt more than a passing attraction for me," I confessed. "I didn't expect it to affect you much."

Savannah stared at me for a long moment. I realized that I couldn't read her as I had before because she had erected barriers around her heart. The knowledge stabbed into my chest like a knife. Savannah had always been completely open with me and now that trust was gone.

"The last time I kissed a man before you was my junior year in college," she admitted quietly. "That was nearly eight years ago. I haven't even been on a date since then, much less kissed someone. You weren't an experiment or a passing fancy. I liked you a lot."

I noticed that everything she said was in past tense and it hit me hard that I might have ruined something special before it had a chance to begin. "I'm sorry, Savannah." She didn't speak and I asked, "Would you like me to leave?"

"No," she replied quickly. "No, I don't want that. I'm just not sure..." She hesitated. "I'm not sure things can be the same."

Though I hated the words, they also gave me hope. She wanted me to stay but she was guarded. Ava had been right when she hinted that my rejection had affected Savannah deeply. I wondered if she was also correct that Savannah and I could find what we both wanted with each other. I wanted to find out.

"Then they'll be different, but I don't necessarily think that's a bad thing."

Savannah looked surprised at my words, but a smile tugged at the corners of her mouth. "You don't think so?"

I shook my head. "We were friends before. This time I'd like to try something different."

The light I'd become so fond of began to return to her eyes. "I don't think you understand what I'm trying to say. I'm not sure I can handle a romantic relationship with you."

"Then we'll date until you do."

"Date?" she asked, her voice high and thin.

"Isn't that what modern couples do when they want to get to know each other? Go to dinner? The movies? Hook up?" I'd heard the last term on television a few days before but I still wasn't completely sure of its meaning.

"Hook up?" Savannah choked, her eyes wide.

"That doesn't mean what I thought it did, does it?"

She laughed, pressing a hand to her stomach. "Hooking up is a euphemism for, well." She paused, a look of consternation on her face.

"Euphemism?" A pretty pink blush spread across her cheeks and I knew she was embarrassed but I wasn't entirely sure why. I couldn't resist teasing her a bit. "What's that?"

She bit her bottom lip. "It's a vague or different way to describe something."

"So what does hooking up describe?"

The pink in her cheeks intensified into a bright red and I began to understand what it meant.

Before I could tell her not to worry about it, she muttered, "Sleeping together. Uh, having sex."

"Okay, maybe that could wait."

Savannah choked again and the blush moved down her neck to her chest. I wanted to kiss her then because she looked so pretty and flustered, but Ava returned to the kitchen, cradling Satchel in her arms like an infant.

"If you two are done having your awkward discussion, could we eat soon?" she asked. "I'm starving and that Salisbury steak smells amazing."

The moment was broken. Savannah turned back to the stove with pink still staining her cheeks. "Yeah, it's nearly ready. I just need to mash the potatoes."

"Then Rhys and I will set the table," Ava volunteered, gesturing for me to go into the dining room. As I walked past her, she whispered, "I'm glad you took my advice. I accept thank you gifts on Tuesdays and Thursdays."

I smiled for the first time in weeks.

CHAPTER TWELVE

Savannah

MY HEART FLUTTERED as I went through the clothes in my closet, trying to find something to wear.

Yesterday, after we ate dinner and Ava left, Rhys stayed behind and helped me wash dishes. Then we lounged on my sofa and I showed him some of my favorite television shows. He was still trying to figure out his new television and the streaming services I'd set up for him.

When it was ten, he declared it was time he went home. I walked him to the front door and he surprised me by lifting my chin with the side of his hand and placing a light kiss on my lips.

"Go to dinner with me tomorrow."

It was an invitation, but not a request. I didn't respond for a moment. I still wasn't sure I was ready to open myself up to him again.

"Savannah," he prompted, his face inches from mine. "Go to dinner with me."

Again, it wasn't a request. His voice had dropped, insistent and nearly a growl.

Deciding I liked this side of Rhys, I nodded as I looked up at him. His answering smile was crooked, a little cocky, and completely unfamiliar. He looked young and maybe even a bit dangerous. The combination was incredibly sexy.

"I'll be here at seven," he stated.

I watched him cross the street to his house and disappear inside before I shut my door. Then I looked at Satchel and clapped my hands in excitement. She jumped and stared at me irritably.

"Mommy has a date with her stupid hot neighbor tomorrow." I thought about my words then. Maybe it was time to stop calling Rhys stupid hot. It sounded a little like I was calling him stupid *and* hot.

Satchel wandered over to the couch and leapt on top of it, settling down with her back to me. Apparently she didn't share my excitement.

Today had flown by because I'd been working at the Bean. Ava offered to help me pick an outfit for tonight, but I had a feeling anything she chose would be more revealing than I was comfortable with. Plus I needed a little time alone before I went out to dinner. Restaurants were tricky for me. They were swarming with emotional ups and downs, couples and families that looked happy enough on the outside but were frustrated, angry, or sad on the inside. It was difficult to maintain my mental shields with so many feelings washing over me. Especially after I'd spent an entire day at work around other people.

I glanced at the clock and decided I was glad Ava had sent me home early. It was nearly six-thirty now and I was still struggling to decide what to wear. On one hand, I had several pretty, flowing maxi dresses that would be comfortable yet lovely for a first date. On the other, I had a flirty black dress that I hadn't worn in years and had completely forgotten about until I'd found it shoved in the very back of my closet. The fit and flare style flattered my curvaceous figure without being too revealing, but it was by far the sexiest thing I owned. It showcased my breasts and legs while hiding what I considered to be my overly ample hips. It was the only piece of sexy clothing I owned and I was torn.

This dress didn't say, "Let's take things slowly." It cried, "Look at me! I'm so sexy!"

Since I couldn't choose, I opted to try on several before I decided, starting with the black dress. I shimmied into it and zipped it, smoothing the material down my hips. As soon as I turned toward the mirror, I knew this was what I was going to wear. The other dresses were pretty, but I wanted to look special on my first real date with Rhys.

Decision made, I slid my feet into my only pair of black pumps. I took a few experimental steps, happy that my ankles didn't turn as I walked. I so rarely wore heels that it was a toss up if I would stroll gracefully or stumble around like a baby deer.

I took the time to touch up my lipstick and tuck a few essentials into a small red clutch. Satchel watched me from the center of my bed then meowed softly, as though she were pleased.

"Thanks, baby," I replied, pretending that she was giving me a compliment rather than luxuriating in my bed.

The butterflies in my stomach intensified when my doorbell rang. I took a deep breath and checked my hair and dress one last time before I went to answer. I was glad I'd gone with the black dress when I saw what Rhys wore. Though we hadn't spent a lot of time together, he usually dressed as though his clothing were an afterthought. Jeans, t-shirts, boots or sneakers, and that was it.

Tonight he wore a dark blue suit that seemed tailored to his frame, emphasizing the breadth of his shoulders and the length of his legs. The color of the suit also emphasized the blue of his eyes.

That thought gave me pause. The first time I met him, his eyes were black as pitch, with no color visible around his pupils. But every time I'd seen him after that they were blue.

I didn't have time to consider that for long because Rhys said, "You look beautiful." His eyes skimmed over me from head to toe and I felt my skin heat in their wake.

"Thank you," I murmured.

"Are you ready to leave?" he asked.

I nodded and stepped out onto the porch, locking the door behind me. When I turned, Rhys reached out and took my hand. The skin of my palm warmed at the contact and I thanked him as he helped me into his SUV.

Once we were inside the vehicle and on our way, I asked, "So where are we going for dinner?"

"The Driskill Grill," he replied.

I stared at him in surprise. The Driskill Grill was a fantastic restaurant inside the Driskill Hotel. It was a lovely spot and a place where a man would take a woman he wanted to impress. I definitely wouldn't feel overdressed there.

Rhys glanced at me. "Is that a problem?"

He looked so concerned that I felt guilty for my reaction. "No, no, not at all. It's just that I've always wanted to go there but for one reason or another I never have."

He smiled. "Then I'm glad to be the one to take you."

As he drove over the South Congress Bridge, I stared out the window. "Can I ask you something?"

"Savannah." His firm tone of voice brought my eyes around to him. He took a moment to look at me. "You don't have to request permission if there's something you want to know about me. Just ask."

I nodded. "Your eyes. The first time I met you they were black, but now they're blue. I was wondering why."

Rhys looked surprised. "They were black the first time we met?"

I nodded. "You didn't know?"

Shrugging, he replied, "They were black...before. But they've been blue for over a year now."

"What happened to change their color?" I asked.

"My brother died."

Those three words were loaded with a wealth of pain and guilt. I wanted to ask more, but now wasn't the time. Instead, I said, "I'm so sorry."

He didn't reply as he steered the SUV through downtown. When he pulled up in front of the Driskill, the valet opened my door and helped me out of the car. A few moments later, Rhys was beside me. His expression was so closed off that my heart sank.

"I'm sorry I asked," I murmured. "I didn't realize it would bring up painful memories."

The stoical mask cracked as he looked down at me. "You couldn't have known, Savannah."

I shrugged as he took my hand. "Yes, but this is our first date and I don't want to ruin it."

His fingers squeezed mine. "I don't think that's possible."

I was too distracted by my thoughts to fully take in the elegant hotel as we made our way into the restaurant, but I managed to snap out of it long enough to appreciate the restaurant. It was dark and dimly lit, the carpet and walls a deep burgundy. Even the ceiling was elegant, covered in beautifully detailed gold panels. We were led to a table that held a single flickering candle in the middle.

All at once I became aware of the buzz of emotion around us. I'd been so distracted by my thoughts that I hadn't taken the time to erect my mental shield in preparation for the onslaught.

Determined to get a handle on myself, I looked around and said, "This is beautiful, Rhys. Thank you for bringing me here."

He smiled. "Would you like a glass of wine?"

"That sounds lovely," I agreed, knowing I wouldn't take more than a few sips. Alcohol made it impossible for me to keep my guard up in such a crowded place.

As we looked over the wine list, more people were led into the dining room, adding to the clamor in my mind. I took a deep breath and closed my eyes, reaching desperately for my mental shields. But they were nowhere to be found.

A thin sheen of sweat spread across my shoulders as I tried to focus, but I was losing the battle.

"Savannah? Are you okay?" Rhys asked quietly.

I shook my head, breathing hard. I could feel the swell of emotion from the couple to our left. The woman was heart broken and the husband was disdainful of her. While I couldn't hear their thoughts, his contempt of her was harsh and cutting, piercing my skull viciously.

The group of men behind us were gloating over some business deal they'd just closed. I could feel their pride and satisfaction that they had managed to screw over their client. All around me, I could see smiling faces and hear laughter, but beneath their facial expressions, there was a seething mass of emotions and most of them were unpleasant in one way or another.

I took a deep breath and tried something that worked from time to time. I reached out around me, searching for one person who was happy or content. Sometimes that was all it would take for me to shore up my defenses.

Unfortunately, it was too late. My breath came faster and faster. I could vaguely hear Rhys and another man speaking, but it didn't penetrate the haze of feelings that enveloped me.

"E-e-xcuse me," I muttered, pushing myself to my feet. "I don't feel well."

I vaguely remembered stumbling from the restaurant, pausing in the hallway outside and planting my hand against the wall to steady myself. I tried to suck in slow, deep breaths to slow the spinning in my head, but nothing worked. Black dots danced in my vision and I couldn't focus my eyes.

I felt a hand on my shoulder. "Savannah?" Rhys asked.

"I-I think I'm going to—" I couldn't fight the darkness any longer as my legs collapsed beneath me.

I never felt the arms that caught me before I hit the floor.

A SMALL WEIGHT settled on my chest, followed by a deep purr. I wanted to reach up and stroke Satchel's back, but my arms didn't cooperate. Something cool and damp swept across my forehead and down my cheek. I tried to turn my face away from it, but the slightly rough fabric followed me.

I moaned and twisted my head the other way.

"Wake up for me, Savannah," Rhys commanded, his voice low and hoarse.

I groaned again, finally able to lift a hand and push the cold cloth away. "I'm awake," I whispered.

"I need you to open your eyes."

"Don't wanna," I complained.

"It's important, Savannah," he insisted.

"Fine." With a sigh, I forced my eyelids open and stared up at his face. "See? I'm awake. Now let me go back to sleep."

A ghost of a smile pulled at his mouth. "I can't let you do that."

"Why not?" I asked grumpily.

"Because you fainted outside The Driskill Grill and I had to carry you to the car. I nearly took you straight to the hospital, but I called Ava first to find the closest one and she told me that you would be fine. That sometimes you did this when you had to deal with crowds." His stare held a hint of reproach.

"I thought it would be okay," I told him. "I haven't gone out in a while, so I forgot how overwhelming it can be. Then I asked you that stupid question that upset you and I didn't take the time to mentally prepare myself."

He leaned back and sighed. "I wasn't upset, Savannah."

I raised my eyebrows and stared at him. "Oh, really?"

Rhys shook his head. "Stop trying to distract me."

"Distract you?"

"You're being sweet and, what's the word? Cute. You're being cute."

"I'm not being cute," I argued, still lying on my back but now scowling at him. "I'm a grown woman. Only children and animals are cute."

I could tell he was biting back a smile, but he managed it. "Whatever you say."

I grunted at him. "This is a ridiculous discussion anyway." I started to push myself up into a sitting position, but his hands came to my shoulders. "I want to sit up," I stated.

"I know, but you should probably wait a few minutes and give yourself time to settle. You went down hard and fast at the restaurant."

"I need caffeine and sugar," I said. "If you'll help me up, I'll make myself a cup of tea with whiskey and honey."

"How about this? You lie here, tell me where everything is, and you can sit up when it's ready."

"Is that a request or an order?" I asked.

"Take it as you like it."

Once again his age was showing in his speech patterns. I didn't know a single man who talked the way he did. "Fine."

He smiled at me and brushed my hair out of my face. "Definitely cute."

I rolled my eyes, which made him laugh. I liked the sound of it and the way his eyes lit up from within when he found something entertaining. Little by little, Rhys was opening up to me.

It dawned on me then that I didn't know his last name. I

thought about that as I lay on the sofa, staring at the ceiling and petting Satchel. I knew very little about him as a person, yet I felt a connection between us. We fit as though we were made to be together. His presence was so comforting, I felt very little of the nerves that plagued me during the beginning of the few relationships I'd had in college.

The fact that I couldn't read Rhys' emotions probably played a part as well. I did often wonder what he was thinking and feeling, but I felt no pressure to meet his unspoken expectations or bend over backwards to please him.

A few minutes later, Rhys returned with two steaming mugs and sat them down on the coffee table. "Ready to sit up?" he asked.

"Yes," I stated firmly.

He smiled again and reached down to help me into a sitting position. My head did one long, lazy spin before my equilibrium settled and I felt somewhat normal. Satchel jumped down off my lap and pranced away, her tail twitching with pride.

Rhys sat down next to me and handed me one of the mugs. I blew on it and took a small sip. Surprisingly, the ratio of whiskey in the tea was perfect.

"You make excellent tea," I commented, taking another sip and letting the hot, alcohol-laced liquid warm me.

"I've had quite a bit of practice."

"What's your last name, Rhys?" I asked, taking another sip.

"The name I'm using now or what I was called when I was made?"

He didn't seem upset by my question, so I said, "Both."

"Right now, all my identification says I'm Rhys Carey, but when Gaius, my creator, made me, I was called The Dark One or Rhys the Dark."

"Because of your eyes?" I asked.

He nodded.

"What was your brother called?" I asked.

Rhys drank down a large swallow of his tea and I wondered if he'd put whiskey in his as well. "The Slayer."

My brows rose. "That doesn't sound good."

He huffed out a bitter laugh. "It wasn't."

I let the topic drop and we drank our tea in silence for a while. When I finished mine, I set the mug to the side and looked at him. "As far as first dates go, I think this one was a little rough."

He grinned at me. "I'd have to agree. Maybe we should consider dates that are less stressful for you," he suggested.

"The only date that would be less stressful is if we stayed here at my house."

"Then that's what we'll do."

I studied him, uncertain of his sincerity. "Are you sure?"

"I'm not interested in what restaurants we go to or movies we see. I'm interested in *you*. I want to know you."

I liked the way he said it. "Okay, then we'll spend time together at my house." Satchel returned to the living room and sat at Rhys' feet, batting his shin with her paw. "And I think Satchel would like that too."

Rhys smiled down at my cat. "I'm looking forward to it." When his eyes returned to mine, a shiver went down my spine. "We'll start tomorrow."

"You could stay and watch a movie with me tonight," I invited.

He shook his head and stood up. "You need to rest. Tomorrow is soon enough."

I rose and followed him to the door. "Thank you for taking care of me tonight," I murmured. "I'm sorry our date was ruined."

He paused, his hand on the doorknob, and looked down at me. "I don't think it was ruined. Though I wish you'd had a chance to eat at the restaurant that you've always wanted to try."

"Maybe another time," I stated, knowing that it probably wouldn't happen.

"Maybe."

We stared at one another for a long moment, neither of us moving. There was a look in his eye I didn't recognize, but it made me feel warm all over. Or maybe that was the whiskey in the tea.

When he leaned down and kissed me gently, I knew that the heat in my belly had nothing to do with whiskey and everything to do with Rhys.

CHAPTER THIRTEEN

Rhys

I GASPED FOR breath and sat straight up in bed. Sweat soaked my body and dampened my hair. My heart hammered against my sternum as though I'd been running for my life. As the dream faded, I shoved my hands through my hair and rested my elbows on my bent knees. My chest heaved as I struggled to catch my breath and fought against the nausea that roiled in my gut.

The bloody, torn remnants of the dream shifted behind my eyelids. It had been clearer than my other nightmares. The gruesome images stayed in my mind even after I woke up, though I wished they would vanish as they had before. In all the time I'd lived, I had never seen anything like the broken bodies of women and children that filled my mind. Such evil was beyond my comprehension.

I rolled out of bed and staggered from the bedroom into the kitchen. I filled a glass with cold water from the tap and drained it in several huge gulps. The nightmares that had plagued me for weeks were coming more often now. Almost nightly. Instead of vaguely unsettling, they were dark and violent, filled with images of blood and pain. This was the worst of them so far, but I was almost certain that it was only the beginning.

A woman who looked a lot like Rhiannon Temple was featured

in most of them. I seemed to be making attempts to seduce her. Pursuing her relentlessly. Though I could clearly hear the words I spoke, they weren't mine. In the nightmares, I offered her anything and everything to share her power with me, telling her that she would be my queen and that we would rule together. It made no sense. When she didn't agree, I threatened her with unspeakable acts. As monstrous as I considered myself, I never would utter threats such as those to a woman.

With each night that passed and each dream I had, I became more and more certain that it was Rhiannon I saw in the dreams and not a woman who resembled her. I also became more convinced that I was experiencing Cornelius' memories. The things I said were similar to the threats I'd heard him utter before.

I wondered what Rhiannon Temple wanted from Savannah or Ava. Or from me. I doubted she'd approached Savannah for business reasons, as she claimed. Especially considering the unique gifts that Savannah had or the massive power that resided within Ava's body. If my suspicions about her were true, the woman was as old as I was, which meant she was no mere human. The fact that my brother had known her and wanted her deepened my anxiety. Cornelius never did anything without a reason. Even when he had killed people, he always had a goal in mind and it usually involved strengthening his own power.

Then there was the fact that I was the last known *animavore*. Soul eaters were once feared and treated like the boogeymen of the supernatural community. Though they were now considered myths because, to my knowledge, Cornelius and I were the only ones. That didn't mean that the lore didn't spread far and wide. The thought of creatures like me was frightening to those who practiced white magic. The dark witches and wizards were in constant pursuit of the knowledge required to make them because legend said that the more souls the *animavore* consumed, the greater his power. If one could take the soul of the *animavore* they would also have his magic.

I knew from experience that this was true. But the magic required to remove the soul eater's power was immense. Very few witches or warlocks in the world could manage it. I'd met one in Dallas and considered her a friend, and another was now my landlord and I very much doubted she wanted my power when her own was likely more potent than mine.

I poured another glass of water and drank this one at a slower pace, carrying it over to the pair of stools that sat next to the kitchen island. I settled on one, taking in the quiet darkness of the house and trying to get my mind off the nightmare that had woken me.

I distracted myself with thoughts of Savannah Baker. Just the memory of my last evening with her was enough to slow my heart rate.

In the two weeks since our first date, I'd spent nearly every evening with Savannah. She would cook or I would bring food and we would talk or watch television. One night she tried to teach me how to play poker. Considering she had to stop and look up the rules several times, that didn't go well, but it was still entertaining. I enjoyed it. Actually, I enjoyed every moment with her. She had the ability to make even the most ordinary activities seem special. Even her silence was comforting.

She was sweet and arousing at the same time. I found myself making an effort to make her laugh because I craved the sound. I often pulled her into my side when we sat on the couch, wrapping an arm around her shoulders and just breathing her in. I wanted her close to me.

Every night, I struggled with the desire to do more than kiss her good-bye, but this wasn't a fling or a quick tumble. I knew she wanted me too, that she wanted me to do more than give her gentle kisses. I could feel her desire, but I was courting this woman and I wanted to take my time. I wasn't so locked in the past that I didn't understand that most people would have had sex by now, but after Savannah admitted to me that her last relationship had been seven years ago, I wasn't going to push her too hard, too fast. I wanted her to trust me completely before we moved to the next step. I didn't want her to regret it later, even if she was eager now.

Even though I tried to ignore the need she emitted, it was difficult. Every time I touched her or kissed her, she would melt against me. Though the weight of her body and the scent of her skin were becoming an addiction, I wanted more from her. I wanted everything she offered me without a word.

But I couldn't take it. Not yet.

In the quiet darkness of the early morning hours, I wondered how I ever thought I could stay away from Savannah Baker. There was so much about her that called to me. Even if Ava hadn't arrived on my doorstep two weeks ago, I would have caved eventually. I would have cracked and ended up knocking on her front door, pleading with her to spend time with me. To speak to me again. In an incredibly short period of time, Savannah had gotten beneath my skin and I doubted she would ever work her way out.

When my mind and body quieted, I put the glass in the sink and walked back to the bedroom. If tonight was like all the others, I would be able to sleep now and the nightmare wouldn't return. Most nights I wouldn't dream again once the nightmare woke me, but sometimes I would dream of Savannah. Of touching her. Kissing her. Making love to her.

Still, even if I couldn't have the reality, my dreams were a welcome if poor substitute.

Tomorrow I would go to *The Magic Bean* and speak to Ava. If my dreams of Rhiannon Temple were anything to go by, danger waited for one, if not both of us in the future and we should be prepared. I hoped that she would have some insight into what was happening to me and what Rhiannon might be up to.

After over two millennia alone, I'd finally found a woman that I could envision a future with and I would not allow anyone or anything to hurt her. I would protect Savannah with everything I had. Including my life.

CHAPTER FOURTEEN

Savannah

"SO, HOW'RE THINGS with Rhys?" Ava asked me casually as we stocked and organized the bookshelves in the Bean.

The afternoon was a slow one, so we were taking the time to tidy the shop and restock books. I was surprised by how neat the witches were when they came into the shop. Everything that they picked up was put back into its proper place if they decided not to buy it. It was rare that a customer left things in disarray.

When I'd mentioned it to Ava, she laughed. "That's because the witches can feel the spell I put on the shelves. If they don't return things to their proper place, there is a price to pay. Typically, it's only the humans who aren't tidy."

"A price to pay?" I asked, my eyes growing larger. "What do you do to them?"

Ava shook her head. "Nothing horrible. But they aren't surprised when their spells go awry for a few days or they need to replace their supply of dried herbs not long after a visit."

"You hex them?" I asked, my voice growing higher.

She laughed again, louder and longer this time. "Not really. It's more of a little spell to throw them off-kilter for a few days. It's harmless." She paused. "Though one witch did come in after she burned her eyebrows off when one of her candle spells didn't go as planned. I had to adjust the charm then."

I shook my head at my friend. "You're a menace. Remind me never to get on your bad side."

"I don't think you could," Ava replied. "Though we might find out if you change the subject again when I ask you about Rhys."

I sighed as I dusted the shelves in front of me. I should have known she would notice that I did that every time she asked me about Rhys and how our dates were going. The truth was I didn't want to tell her because I wasn't sure I even knew what was going on.

For the past several weeks, Rhys came over to my house every day. Most of the time it was in the evening after I finished working for the day. Sometimes he came just after lunch and helped me in the garden when I was only at the Bean for the morning shift. I enjoyed his company and looked forward to seeing him every day, but his behavior confused me.

Rhys wasn't overly affectionate. He only held my hand from time to time and often when we sat on the couch watching television, he'd put his arm around my shoulders, but that was it. His hands and eyes never wandered. Surprisingly, I wanted them to. I wanted him to touch me and I definitely wanted to touch him. I found nearly everything about him attractive, from his endearing lack of understanding of pop culture to his not-quite-dimples. For the first time in years, my libido was awake and raring to go. Too bad he didn't seem to get the memo, even though I knew he had to feel my desire for more.

If it hadn't been for the kisses he gave me each night before he left, I would have thought that maybe we were just friends. But even the kisses were somewhat chaste. Rhys always kept the contact brief and his hands never strayed from my waist.

For the first time in my life, I was dating a man who took old-fashioned values seriously. My grandmother would have been ecstatic.

However, I was ready for more. Maybe not sex, but definitely some making out or a groping session on my couch. I felt like I was back in high school and my boyfriend wouldn't touch me because he was afraid my parents would come down the hall and catch us.

"Savannah, are you going to answer my question or am I going to have to get out my hex book?"

I blinked at Ava. "Sorry. I was thinking."

"I could tell. I think I smell smoke, so whatever it is must be serious."

I made a face at her insinuation. "My brain isn't overheating, I'm just a little…confused about what I should do about Rhys."

"Well, why don't you talk to me about it and I'll tell you what I think you should do."

I laughed. "You may be my boss here at the Bean, but my private life is my own," I retorted.

"Wrong. I may be your boss here, but I'm also your best friend, which means you have to at least consider my suggestions," she corrected.

Still laughing, I shook my head. "No, I don't."

"Okay, no you don't," she sighed. "But I'm dying of curiosity, so please put me out of my misery. I know you think it's rude to kiss and tell or whatever, but I feel like I had a bit of a hand in getting you two together. I need details."

"Something would have to happen for me to kiss and tell," I muttered to myself as I dusted the candles on their shelves.

"What did you just say?" Ava asked.

I glanced at her. "You heard me."

"Okay, back up. Instead of saying something would have to happen, why don't you tell me what has happened so far?"

I tossed my dust rag into the plastic basket of cleaning supplies.

"We spend time together. We eat dinner or watch TV. Then he leaves."

"That's it?" Ava asked. "No fooling around or anything?" She sounded shocked.

"Well, he does kiss me good night before he leaves, but that's it."

"One kiss?" Now she seemed horrified. "No groping or dry humping or anything?"

I made another face at her reference to dry humping and she rolled her eyes. "Don't knock it till you've tried it."

Considering I'd never dry humped before and didn't have any plans to start now, I let the subject drop. "No, nothing other than one kiss."

"Does he at least slip you the tongue?" she asked.

"Ava!" I cried out, twisting toward her. "I can't believe you asked me that."

"What? The way you put it, he's acting more like your BFF than your BF."

I made a face at her. "BF as in best friend or boyfriend?" I asked.

"Boyfriend, Savannah," she replied, clearly exasperated with my joking.

"I think he's trying to take things slowly," I stated.

"Probably, but there's a difference between smart slow and glacier slow. A kiss with tongue isn't exactly scandalous in this day and age."

She did have a point, but we didn't have a chance to debate it because the bell over the door to the shop rang and we both turned to face the customers.

Rhiannon Temple stood just inside the door. As she had before, she looked sophisticated and sleek, her long black hair hung in a straight sheet to her waist. She wore a royal blue sheath that hugged her slender figure. Over her forearm, she looped a handbag that carried a discreet triangular label that I recognized. A tall man loomed over her, his broad body dwarfing her though her heels put her nearly at the same height. He was large and muscular and he looked as though he belonged on a calendar for sexy bad boys on motorcycles.

"Hello," she said, coming deeper into the shop. Her eyes flicked to me. "It's nice to see you again, Savannah," she greeted as she held a hand out to me.

Though I didn't want to shake her hand, I took her fingers and released them as quickly as possible. Touching her skin made me feel chilled all over.

"Hello," I replied.

Rhiannon turned to Ava. "Hello, you must be Ava Amaris." She reached into her bag and removed a small cream-colored card. "I'm Rhiannon Temple and I'm a property developer and real estate agent in Austin. I stopped by several of your rental properties in Travis Heights and I would be very interested talking to you about them."

Ava took the card but didn't spare it a glance. "May I offer you and your…friend a coffee?" she asked, neither confirming nor denying Rhiannon's assumption that she was Ava Amaris.

"That sounds lovely, thank you. I'll take a nonfat cappuccino," Rhiannon said with a small toss of her head. Her black hair rippled before settling back against her spine, moving as though it had a life of its own. I wasn't sure why but the sight of her hair falling perfectly into place made me wonder if perhaps she was a witch. It was almost as if the strands rearranged themselves until they were completely smooth.

Ava's eyes shifted to the man behind Rhiannon. "Can I get you something…" she trailed off.

"My name is Macgrath," the man replied. "And I don't want

anything."

His voice was rough and low, as though he didn't use it often. Ava nodded and turned to me.

"Savannah, would you mind?"

Sensing the undercurrents of tension in the room, I hurried behind the counter, unsure of what I should do. Unlike Ava, I had no magical abilities and for some reason, I felt as though I might need them. My intuition wasn't as strong as a witch's, but it was twanging sharply at the moment, warning me that there was danger here. Mostly because the few emotions that radiated from the others were defensive or hostile. There was also an underlying sense of smugness but I couldn't quite tell where it emanated from.

Quickly I made a medium nonfat cappuccino, putting it into a paper to-go cup. When I carried it to Rhiannon, she took it without a word of thanks, which only solidified my vague aversion for her into concrete dislike. My gaze flicked to Macgrath behind her and I found his gaze on me.

Disturbed by the way he was looking at me I lowered my own eyes and walked over to the shelves next to Ava. I began putting away the cleaning products, loading everything in the basket just to keep my hands busy.

"Why are you interested in my rental properties?" Ava asked Rhiannon.

The woman took a sip of the cappuccino before she answered. "I'd like to buy them from you," she stated. "You own several homes on the same block and I'm interested in refurbishing them for resale. I would, of course, offer you fair market value for them."

Ava crossed her arms over her chest, studying Rhiannon closely. "Thank you for your offer, but I'm not interested in selling at this time."

The real estate agent's mouth thinned at Ava's words and I

noticed that Macgrath smirked behind her, as though he were pleased that she had been thwarted.

"Are you sure? Perhaps an extra twenty percent on the purchase price would change your mind?"

Ava shook her head. "No, it wouldn't."

Once again I saw her eyes move to Macgrath. He met her gaze with an implacable stare and the strange tension in the room intensified tenfold.

"You seem like an intelligent woman," he said to Ava suddenly.

She tilted her head to the side and narrowed her eyes at him. "I believe I am."

"Then perhaps you should think about her offer."

I nearly choked at the thinly veiled threat and twisted my head to look at Ava.

My insane boss threw her head back and laughed. "What is this, a mob movie?" she asked. "Will there be a horse head in my bed tomorrow morning?"

Strangely enough, the corners of Macgrath's mouth twitched as though he found Ava's complete lack of fear amusing. He grinned and I watched in horror as his canine teeth extended and his eyes began to glow. He was a vampire.

Ava merely shook her head. "Your parlor tricks don't frighten me, vampire, so save the theatrics."

His grin widened but his teeth receded back. "Of course not."

The door behind him opened, but he didn't react, which made me wonder if he'd heard the person approaching before they arrived. I glanced around him and saw Rhys. Macgrath turned then and looked Rhys up and down.

"Excuse me," Rhys murmured, stepping inside and letting the door shut behind him.

Without a word, Macgrath moved to his left. Rhiannon had turned when Rhys spoke and now she was smiling at him in a way that I didn't like. At all. Her gaze was very nearly predatory.

"Nice to see you again, Rhys," she greeted him.

He nodded to her. "Ms. Temple."

"Oh, please, call me Rhiannon," she invited him, placing a hand on his arm.

Rhys' eyes came to mine and I watched as their color changed, the blue of his irises quickly swallowed by the black of his pupil. Within seconds the whites were encompassed as well, leaving his eyes black as night.

Next to me, Ava went stiff and I knew she saw it. Rhys stepped away from Rhiannon so that her hand fell away. He blinked several times and when he looked up once again, his eyes had returned to blue.

It was clear to me that he was suspicious of her because he didn't turn his back on her as he moved across the shop toward me. Though he didn't usually hug or kiss me when we saw each other, he took the time to press his lips lightly to mine then wrapped his arm around my waist, settling me into his side. His actions alone told me everything I needed to know. He didn't trust Rhiannon Temple and he intended to protect me should it become necessary. There was a fine tension in his muscles that told me he was on his guard.

"Well, thank you for stopping by, Rhiannon," Ava said politely. "But I don't think I'll be selling my properties anytime soon."

The real estate agent smiled thinly, her dark eyes sparkling with challenge. "Well, you have my card if you change your mind."

With that, she turned and walked out the door, not even waiting to see if Macgrath followed her. I watched as he paused, his eyes on Ava, and he looked as though he were about to say something. Instead, his mouth tightened and he walked out of the shop.

As soon as the door shut behind them, Ava turned to us. "You know that witch?" she asked, her voice strained.

"Not really. She came by the house about a month ago, asking if I would want to sell it. I told her that you were my landlord and where to find you. When you didn't mention it, I assumed she called or came by and you told her you weren't interested," I answered.

"Why didn't you mention it?"

I glanced over at Rhys. "Well, I was a bit distracted after her visit." The day Rhys had taken me to the botanical gardens was also the day Rhiannon had stopped by the house. My heart had ached so badly that I hadn't given Rhiannon another thought until today.

Ava nodded. "It's okay. You couldn't have known."

"Known what?" Rhys asked.

"That she's a witch. A very powerful, dark witch."

"How do you know that?" I asked.

"It's all over her. Her aura is pitch black and filled with evil."

Rhys stiffened beside me. "I couldn't see it."

Ava shook her head. "You wouldn't have been able to, neither of you, even with your abilities. As I said, she's powerful and she's taken the time and energy to cloak as much of her evil as she can. The only reason I can see it is because of a spell I placed on the shop. As soon as she walked in, everything she tried to hide was fully revealed." Ava paced across the center of the room. "She's dangerous, but I'm not sure if she intends to harm us or if we're just a means to an end. Either way, she's bad news."

"Then we need to be ready," Rhys stated.

Ava stopped her manic movements. "Oh, we will be."

"There's something I need to discuss with both of you," he continued. "But not here. Meet me at the house in half an hour and we'll talk."

Ava nodded. "Take Savannah with you. I'll be there as soon as

I close up."

"You may need me," I argued. "What if they come back?"

This time when Ava looked at me, I saw something in her I'd never seen before—anger, determination, and ice-cold control. She was no longer my warm, loving friend. She was a warrior. A goddess prepared for battle.

"Then they'll have to deal with me."

CHAPTER FIFTEEN

Rhys

S AVANNAH WAS SILENT on the walk to my house. As we
approached, she turned to look across the street.

"We should get Satchel," she stated. "She'll be upset if she sees
me and I don't go inside."

I followed her gaze and saw the little gray cat perched in the
window, watching us. "Let's go get her then."

A few moments later, we were within the safety of my house,
Satchel cuddled close to Savannah's chest. The cat seemed to sense
that her mistress needed her because it curled closer to Savannah,
purring incessantly.

While we waited for Ava to arrive, I took the time to brew
some tea. I didn't have Irish whiskey, but I did put a dollop of
bourbon in each cup and wrapped the teapot in a towel to keep it
warm after I poured out a measure for Savannah and myself.

I carried the tea back into the living room and gave one mug to
Savannah. "It's hot and it's got a dash of bourbon in it," I warned
her, concerned at the way her freckles stood out against her pale
skin.

Without a word, she took a sizeable sip. She gasped after she
was done, setting the cup on the coffee table while she tried to
catch her breath.

"I warned you," I said.

Savannah nodded. "I know, but I really needed that." Her eyes lifted to mine. "I've never experienced anything like what happened in the shop today. There were so many veiled threats and underlying emotions flying around that I couldn't focus on a single one. I'm not even sure what's going on. The only thing I understood clearly was that Rhiannon wants something from us, but I have no clue what that could be."

I took a drink from my cup. After I swallowed down the brew of caffeine and liquor, I replied, "I may know the answer to that."

Savannah looked at me in surprise. "You do? What is it?"

"Let's wait for Ava. I'd prefer to tell both of you at the same time." I drank more tea, let the warmth of the bourbon warm me, and took a deep breath. "But I'm afraid you won't like me very much when I'm done."

Her brows lowered. "I doubt that could happen."

I set my cup aside before I gave in to the temptation to drain it. I needed all my wits about me for the conversation to come. Then, after Savannah and Ava were staring at me in disgust, I would drink.

"I've lived for a very long time, Savannah," I began. "I've done things that most people can't even fathom. Things I'm not proud of and even more that I wish I could forget."

She stroked a hand down Satchel's back, whether in an effort to comfort the cat or herself, I wasn't sure. "Well, let me decide how I feel about your past before you make up your mind for me, okay?"

I smiled at her. That was one of the things I admired most about Savannah. She very rarely judged. It was refreshing to encounter a woman like that. With her empathic abilities, she saw clearly into the root of the emotions people around her experienced. She understood how other people felt in a way that most people could not because she shared in their suffering, joy, or anger. Because of that, she said she couldn't be upset with people over how they felt. Most people never had an opportunity to walk in someone else's shoes, but Savannah did it on a daily basis with grace and generosity of spirit.

The doorbell rang and Savannah jumped.

"It's okay. It's Ava," I said.

"I know, I'm just on edge," she replied with a sigh.

When I let Ava into the house, she appeared much calmer and in complete control.

"Everything okay?" I asked as I shut the door behind her.

She nodded. "Fine. They left and didn't return." When she saw the mugs of tea we were drinking, she asked, "May I have some of that tea?"

"With bourbon or without?"

"With. Definitely with."

I could hear the murmur of their voices as I made Ava a cup of tea. I wasn't looking forward to what I had to tell them. I knew it would change the way they both saw me. I wasn't ready to share the story, but I had no other choice. It was becoming obvious that my dreams were harbingers and ignoring the signs would only put us in more danger.

I tucked the bourbon beneath one arm and carried the teapot and Ava's cup into the living room.

She smiled as she took the mug. "Thank you."

After I refilled my cup and Savannah's mug, there was nothing left to do. Nothing to keep me from telling them what they needed to hear.

With no clue where to begin I sat down in the chair where I liked to read.

As usual, Ava seemed to see through me. "What did you want to talk to us about?" she prompted. "I'm assuming it has something to do with Rhiannon."

"It does," I answered. "But first I need to tell you a story about two brothers. Identical twins." I paused, gathering my thoughts. "They were born into slavery a long, long time ago. Though their lives were hard, they found happiness where they could. Until they were ten. Their master could no longer afford to keep them both and rather than separate them, he sold them at a slave market. With their blond hair and blue eyes, they were much sought after. After a great deal of haggling, they were sold to a very wealthy man with certain...proclivities." I stopped speaking then, fighting back memories that should have faded with the thousands of years that had passed since that time. "The next twelve years were difficult. Even after the boys became too old to interest the man in the way they once did, he had other uses for them. He was a warlock, you see, determined to discover the secret to eternal life. Eternal youth. His experiments were often painful and lasted for days. Finally, when they boys had become young men, he was successful. He turned one twin first, nearly killing him in the process. He was in agony for days. And when he finally recovered, he wasn't the same. He carried evil in his core. But their master learned from his mistakes the first time. He refined the process over the next few months. Then he came for the other twin and changed him as well."

I paused in the story then. I didn't want to tell them what happened next, but they had to know so they could understand what was to come.

"After he turned the second brother, the first managed to escape and killed their master. The second brother thought he would be free, but he was wrong. He was no longer a slave but he was still a prisoner. For centuries, he would try to escape his brother but it was impossible. The first brother would find him and the experiments and cruelty would continue. Until finally the second could take no more. He knew that his only choice was to die or kill the only family he had left. So he studied and planned for his kind were nearly impossible to destroy. When he succeeded in killing his brother, he grieved, but there was also relief. He was no longer under the thumb of madness. But there were unintended side effects."

Throughout the story, I couldn't meet either of the women's eyes. I wasn't sure what I would see when they looked at me, but now I couldn't avoid it any longer. I looked to Ava first, expecting to see anger and disgust. Instead I saw compassion and understanding.

Her reaction was unexpected, but it didn't prepare me for what I saw when my eyes moved to Savannah. She sat on the couch, her cup clutched in her hands and tears in her eyes.

I couldn't understand why she was crying for me. I had just revealed that I killed my brother, an unforgivable act, yet she looked sad instead of repulsed.

"What side effects?" Ava asked, drawing my attention away from Savannah.

I cleared my throat. "The only way to kill him was to take his soul, and the souls he stole, into my body. I didn't understand at the time what it would do to me. I see things, usually in my sleep. They're memories, but the memories aren't my own. They belong to Cornelius. That's how I know Rhiannon is dangerous. Since she came to Savannah's house a few weeks ago, I've been dreaming of her. At first I thought it was a trick of the mind. That I inserted her into my dreams because there was something about her I didn't like, but after a while I realized that wasn't the case. That's why I came into the store today. I wanted to talk to you about it, but she was there. Then you said that she practiced dark magic and I knew for certain that she had something to do with how Cornelius and I were made."

Ava's eyes narrowed. "What do you mean?"

"In my dreams, she was there the night Cornelius was made. She helped Gaius create us. She wasn't there when I was changed, but Gaius never would have been able to succeed if it weren't for her." I took a deep breath. "Then throughout Cornelius' memories she appears again and again. He wanted something from her. Something she wouldn't give him willingly. Now that he's dead, she no longer has to worry about his pursuit and she can continue with whatever she had planned before."

Ava nodded, her expression thoughtful. "That sounds plausible, but we can't count on it," she stated. "Each of us is unique in our own right and Rhiannon approached Savannah first. For all we know, it's Savannah she wants. Or me."

She made an excellent point. "I'm not sure I'll be content to watch and wait."

Ava frowned at me. "I wouldn't be either, but we also need to learn as much as we can about her before we do anything. It's clear that she's been watching us for a while and we have no idea what she truly wants."

"Power," Savannah interjected, her voice dreamy as though her mind were far away. "She hides her emotions well, but the desire for power is the strongest. She wants to be respected, no, revered, and the only way to accomplish that is to have power." Savannah blinked and her gaze refocused on us. "I couldn't sense anything else from her at the shop except that."

"What about Macgrath?" Ava asked.

Savannah shook her head. "I've never seen anything like him. It's almost as if his heart is encased in stone. There is no getting in there."

Ava nodded. "Well, I will contact my friends in the area and see what they know about Rhiannon Temple."

"I have a friend I can call as well," I stated.

"We'll talk again in a few days. Until then, be careful and call me immediately if Rhiannon comes back," Ava commanded. She got to her feet and set her mug on the coffee table. "Rhys, could I speak to you privately for a moment?"

I followed her outside onto the front porch, shutting the door behind me. Ava gestured for me to walk with her to her car. When we were a few feet from the house, she stopped and turned toward me. "I want you to keep an eye on Savannah. She can protect herself, but she never would because she cannot stand the pain it causes if she hurts someone. That means you and I are responsible for protecting her."

I nodded. "I fully intend to."

"I assumed you would, but it made me feel better to say it anyway," she replied with a sigh.

"You care for her a great deal, don't you?" I asked.

"She is like a little sister to me. I love her," she replied simply.

"I'll protect her," I vowed. "Because I couldn't bear it if anything happened to her either."

Ava nodded. "I'll call you in a few days."

With that, she climbed into her car and left. I returned to the house and found Savannah going through my refrigerator, taking out food and setting it on the counter.

"I hope you don't mind," she said when she saw me. "But I'm hungry and I thought I would make dinner."

"I'll help," I offered.

She smiled at me and we worked together to prepare the meal. I didn't have much in the way of food since I spent most of my time at Savannah's house, but we made do.

"I don't think badly of you," she said suddenly as she stirred the vegetables she was cooking. "About your brother, I mean."

My hands paused in seasoning the chicken I was planning to grill, but I didn't speak.

"You're a very hard man to read emotionally, but I could still sense your guilt and your grief over his death," she continued, her eyes on the pan in front of her. "I know it wasn't a decision you wanted to make and you clearly avoided it for as long as possible."

"Why do you say that?"

Finally, her dark eyes lifted and met mine. "You waited over two thousand years to kill him, Rhys. I think that was ample opportunity for him to change his ways or let you go. The fact that he didn't do either of those things tells me you had no choice." Her voice grew softer. "And maybe it's wrong of me to think this, but if you hadn't stopped him, he would have killed you and you wouldn't be here with me now."

Neither of us spoke much after that as we finished preparing the meal. I wasn't sure what to say and Savannah seemed to be lost in her own thoughts. I wanted to give her time to come to terms with whatever preyed on her mind.

After we ate, I insisted on washing the dishes.

"I want to help," Savannah said.

"Then sit on the counter next to me and drink your wine."

She sighed but did as I asked, hopping up to sit on the counter a few feet from the sink, a glass of wine in her hand. She didn't speak for a while as she watched me wash the pans and plates from our dinner.

"You aren't going to stop speaking to me again, are you?" she asked suddenly, her voice small.

"What do you mean?"

"When we kissed the first time, you stopped speaking to me for weeks. You aren't going to do that again now, right?"

She sounded so uncertain that I could have whipped myself for doing that to her.

"No, I'm not letting you go unless you ask me to," I answered, my hands clenched beneath the soapy dishwater. I wanted to grab her and show her exactly how much I wanted her.

"Good," she whispered.

When all the dishes were washed, I walked Savannah and Satchel back to her house. This time, when she opened the door, I did something I hadn't before. I walked through her house to check each room and the windows and doors. I wanted to be sure she was safe.

Even after I'd ascertained that her home was secure, I didn't want to leave. I might be right across the street, but it would take time to reach her if she needed me.

"Thank you," she said when I returned to the living room where she waited by the front door.

"For what?"

"Making sure that I'm safe."

I approached her and brushed her cheek with the tips of my fingers. "I will always keep you safe if you want," I replied.

She smiled. "As a modern, independent woman, I think I'm supposed to tell you thanks but no thanks, but I guess I'm a failure at that. I like that you want to keep me safe."

"Just because I wish to be the one to ensure your safety doesn't make you any less capable of doing it yourself. When you care about someone, you want to protect them from harm."

I leaned down and pressed my lips to hers. Each night, it grew more and more difficult to leave after a single kiss, but tonight wasn't the time to give in to those urges. Savannah needed time to think about everything I said today, whether she realized it or not.

When I lifted my head, she surprised me by reaching up and wrapping one hand around the back of my neck while the other sank into my hair. Then she pulled me back down, her mouth insistent and hungry against my own.

I couldn't resist the demand she made and opened my lips over hers. Our tongues tangled together and her fingers fisted against my scalp, tugging at my hair.

I crowded her, pushing her back against the front door until our bodies were melded together. Savannah moaned into my mouth, her back arching. Her hands released my neck and hair and moved down my shoulders and chest.

I grabbed her wrists, pinning them to the door next to her head, but never lifted my mouth from hers. She twisted against me, trying to free her hands, but I couldn't release her. If she touched me again, I wouldn't be able to stop myself from taking what she offered.

Finally, she relaxed against me and I let go of her wrists in order to lace our fingers together. In slow degrees, the kiss calmed until I felt more in control. This time, when I lifted my mouth from hers, Savannah didn't struggle. She stared up at me, her dark eyes heavy-lidded and her chest rising and falling with her rapid breathing.

"What are you doing to me, Savannah?" I asked her, our faces close.

"I'm trying to make you mine," she whispered.

"I think it's too late for that," I told her. "Because I'm already yours."

CHAPTER SIXTEEN

Savannah

D ESPITE MY WORRY about what was happening with Rhiannon, I still felt as though I were walking on air. It had been three days since Rhys told me that he was mine. Since that night, things between us had changed.

He spent even more time with me. He drove me to work and picked me up, then he spent the rest of the day and evening with me until it was time for bed. Only then would he leave and return to his house.

I knew it was his way of protecting me from the threat Rhiannon and Macgrath presented but I still liked it.

Other things changed as well. Each day, he grew a little more affectionate. He would touch my hair or my waist often, just a brush of his hand or a light caress. His kisses were no longer short or light. And he kissed me often.

Just the memory of his mouth on mine and his hands on my body made my knees weak. He was different now. He was no longer holding himself back with me, at least not completely.

As I showered and got ready for the day, I wondered how it would turn out. Ava closed the Bean on Sundays, saying that even she needed a day off every week. Rhys invited himself over last night, saying he would like to spend the day with me. When I told him I planned to spend the morning in the garden, he didn't even blink. He offered to help me.

I wanted to see how he handled tending the plants and flowers that I loved so much. I also wondered if he would find it as relaxing as I did.

I dressed quickly in light cotton pants and a tank top and tied my damp hair up in a bun. When I entered the kitchen, the coffee pot was already full since I set the timer the night before. As soon as I poured a cup, the doorbell rang. Quickly, I made another mug of coffee and carried it with me when I went to answer the door.

"Good morning," I greeted Rhys, noting the dark circles beneath his eyes. I hated that he wasn't sleeping and wished there was something I could do about it. Well, I knew what we could do that would help us both sleep, but I couldn't see myself issuing that invitation verbally. I felt heat creeping up my chest and neck at the direction my thoughts took. I held out the coffee mug. "I made coffee."

He smiled warmly at me and took the cup. "Thank you."

Though it was early morning, the day was already beginning to warm up. Austin in the summer could get hot during the day, so we needed to get moving if we wanted to be done in the garden before the temperatures reached sweltering levels.

"Do you want some toast or something?" I asked him, shutting the door after he walked inside.

He shook his head as he sipped the coffee. "No, thanks."

"Then we should probably get started before it gets to hot."

We each drank a cup of coffee and Rhys followed me outside. Throughout the morning, I asked him to help me weed beds and trim dead blooms from plants in the front. Then I led him into the backyard to do the same. By the time we were done, the sun was high in the sky and my stomach was growling.

I took a few moments to gather herbs from the kitchen garden

I'd planted near the back door and carried them inside. My shirt and pants were dusty and my hands were grimy from hours spent working in the dirt. Rhys was in a similar state.

"Why don't we clean up, then have lunch?" I asked.

Rhys looked down at himself. "I probably do need to clean up and change."

After he left, I scrubbed my hands and arms in the kitchen sink. When I finished, I walked back into the bedroom and decided to jump in the shower and rinse off. Rhys implied he was going to do the same before he left, so I should have plenty of time.

Leaving my hair pinned up, I quickly washed my body and face in the shower, rinsing the remnants of sweat and dirt from my skin. I dried off and slipped into clean underwear. I was picking out a dress from my closet when I heard a sound behind me. Since the latch was old and rarely caught properly, I assumed it was Satchel shoving the door open, as was her habit. She hated being locked out of my bedroom.

"Just a minute, Satchel," I said. "Mommy needs to get dressed before you go opening the door."

I turned around and froze, clutching the garment to the front of my body. Rhys stood in the doorway, his eyes hot and a little wild. My mouth went dry at the expression on his face and I couldn't speak.

"I'm sorry," he muttered, stepping back. "The door was open and..." he trailed off. "I'll wait for you in the living room."

He disappeared down the hallway as I stood unmoving in front of my closet. I carried the dress into my bathroom and shut myself in. My skin felt scorched where his eyes had traveled and I looked at myself in the mirror, wondering for just a moment if his gaze had left marks on my body with its heat.

My pale skin was flushed and the blush darkened when I realized I was wearing a white bra and pale pink lace panties that revealed nearly as much as they covered. I might as well have been naked. I pulled the dress over my head and took my hair down from its bun and brushed it. When it was smooth, I braided it so that the tail fell over my left shoulder.

I debated putting on make-up but realized that I was just trying to kill time before I faced Rhys. I took a deep breath and blew it out slowly. I was being silly. Just a few days ago, I was thinking about how much I wanted Rhys to touch me and how eager I was to make love. I wouldn't be able to share that with him if I freaked out about the idea of him seeing me naked.

Feeling calmer, I left my bedroom and found Rhys in the kitchen with his phone to his ear and his back to me.

"So there's nothing you can tell me about her?" he asked. He paused, listening to the person on the other end. "I know Austin isn't that close to Dallas, Kerry, but this witch is powerful. Someone, somewhere, would have known her or dealt with her." His shoulders tensed as he let the other person respond. "No, I understand what you're saying. I'm just frustrated because Rhiannon is here and it's clear she has an agenda that involves at the very least me, and maybe the woman I care about. I need answers and no one can give them to me." There was another pause. "Okay, thank you. I appreciate that. I'll be waiting for your call." Then he laughed. "I told you that you owed me nothing, Kerry, and I meant it, but if it makes you feel better I'll say it. This makes us even."

He said good-bye and disconnected the call before he turned around. As soon as he saw me, his eyes heated. "I'm sorry about earlier," he said. "I didn't mean to invade your privacy."

I shrugged. "It's okay. It was an accident." I didn't add that I hoped he would eventually be seeing a lot more of me than that anyway. "Who were you talking to?" I asked.

"A friend of mine in Dallas. Her name is Kerry."

"How do you know her?"

"It's a long story," he replied. "And I'm hungry. Why don't we go pick up some lunch and I'll tell you about it while we eat?"

We took his car to pick up Thai food for lunch. When we returned to my house, I set the table in the breakfast nook and we sat down to eat.

"So how did you meet Kerry?" I asked as we put rice and curry on our plates.

Rhys' expression darkened. "It has to do with my brother and how he died," he answered.

I put my hand on his. "I'm sorry." I almost suggested that we talk about it later, but he began speaking again, as though he wanted to get it off his chest.

"Kerry is a witch and the High Priestess of her coven. Cornelius was creating problems for her and her friends in Dallas. I offered to help them because there was no way either of us could defeat Cornelius on our own. After my brother was dead, I thought that it was over, but Kerry isn't the type of woman to let things go. Everywhere I went she was able to find me."

"She stalked you?" I asked in confusion.

Rhys smiled. "No, not exactly. She extended her friendship." He lifted his hand and hooked a finger in the chain around his neck, pulling an amulet from beneath his shirt. "Until she sent me this, I couldn't drive a car or use a cell phone. Electronics and appliances don't work properly when I'm around. It's something about the way I'm made." He considered the amulet for a moment. "I think she felt indebted to me."

"Or maybe she just wanted to be your friend," I replied.

He looked confused by my statement. "Why?"

Even though I forced my mouth to smile, my heart broke for him a little. "Because you're a good man, Rhys. You helped them when they needed you."

"But I also used them to help myself," he argued.

Rhys was so determined to see himself in the worst possible light. "It's okay to have relationships that are mutually beneficial, Rhys. The fact that Kerry still wanted to talk to you after it was over says a lot about her feelings toward you."

He studied me for a moment. "I've never met a woman like you before," he said, his gaze intense.

"I'm taking that as a compliment," I replied.

Smiling, he shot back, "You should because that's how I meant it."

"So how is Kerry going to help us with the Rhiannon situation?"

"I was hoping she would know something about her or at least find someone who does," Rhys answered. "But so far no one knows anything about her."

"It's only been three days," I pointed out. "And she's very good at hiding in plain sight. It will just take some time to find someone who knows her."

"Maybe," Rhys replied.

Ready to change the subject, I asked, "If you couldn't drive a car before Kerry sent you the amulet, how did you learn to drive?"

"I watched," he replied.

I stared at him in surprise. "So you really hadn't driven before the test drive at the dealership?" I asked. We had discussed this before, but I hadn't truly believed him.

Rhys grinned. "Not really."

"That explains a lot," I grumbled beneath my breath.

"What does that mean?"

Shit, he'd heard me. "Uh, n-n-nothing really," I stammered.

He lifted his brows at me. "What does that explain?" he prompted again.

I sucked in a breath and decided to be honest. "Well, uh, I might have prayed to the goddess to protect me from an early death or serious injury when you were driving the SUV for the first time."

Rhys laughed and I was glad to see the last of the darkness fade from his expression. "I'm sure I've improved since then," he murmured.

I suddenly became very interested in eating my curry, which made him laugh again, but he dropped the subject.

We finished our meal and he helped me carry everything into the kitchen. As I loaded the dishwasher, I asked, "What do you want to do this afternoon?"

"Why don't we watch that movie you've been telling me about?" he suggested. "Or take a nap."

I laughed. "Take a nap?"

"Gardening is a lot more work than I thought," he replied, smirking.

"Well, I'll turn on the movie and if you fall asleep, I'll change the channel."

"Sounds fair," he agreed.

When we settled on the couch and turned on the TV, Rhys put his arm around me, pulling me against his side. His hand trailed over my bare arm in a slow up and down motion, making me very aware of the fact that he'd seen me nearly naked just an hour ago.

I tilted my head back to say something to him and found his eyes on my legs, which were left mostly bare by the loose skirt of my dress. He lifted his eyes and our gazes clashed. I lifted a hand to cup his cheek. "Rhys," I whispered, unsure of how to ask for what I wanted.

Somehow, he understood and lowered his head. Our lips met and the heat flared between us immediately. Our tongues danced in a slow, sensuous rhythm. His opposite arm came around my waist, his hand splayed over my hip. I shifted against him, eager for his touch.

Surprising myself with my own boldness, I swung my leg over his lap and straddled him, settling onto his thighs. Rhys immediately accepted the invitation I presented and one of his palms moved up my legs beneath my dress. I shivered at the sensation of his bare skin against mine. The calluses on his fingers were a rough caress and I wanted more.

My hips moved against his lap as his fingertips brushed the edge of my lace underwear. His other had cupped my breast through my dress and I arched deeper into the touch. His fingers delved beneath my dress and bra and slipped over my nipple. I gasped into his mouth, feeling my nipple tighten and tingle from the contact.

I wanted to touch him as well and I reached down between us and lifted the hem of his t-shirt. My fingers brushed the heated flesh of his abdomen and the muscles of his thighs tensed beneath me. Smoothing my hands up his torso and over his chest, I used the motion to lift his shirt higher. He released me long enough for me to tug the garment over his head.

Suddenly, the lamps flickered and I was thrown into a raging sea of emotions that were not my own. Desire, desperation, and love wrapped around me with such intensity that it stole my breath and blurred my vision. Beneath the passion, I could sense loss, loneliness, and guilt. It was a maelstrom that sucked me beneath the surface.

My hands reached out blindly, coming into contact with the bare flesh of Rhys' shoulders. "Rhys," I gasped.

"Fuck," he swore, catching me before I could slide off his lap into a heap on the floor. Holding me with one arm, I could feel his body jerking as he reached out for something with the other.

The sound of a small explosion reached my ears and my vision dimmed further. Rhys swore again, his search becoming more frantic.

Then, just as suddenly as it began, the wild squall of emotions ended and I collapsed against Rhys' naked chest. Breathing heavily, I reached up and curved my hand around his neck, feeling the wild throb of his pulse against my fingers. The cool, thin chain of his amulet shifted beneath my hand and I realized that it had come off when I removed his shirt. Apparently the amulet did more than create a barrier for the electrical disruption that Rhys' powers caused. It also prevented an empath from sensing his emotions.

I was overwhelmed by the immense weight of the pain and sorrow he carried. More than once since I met him, I often wished I could feel what Rhys was feeling, sense where his mind was. Now that I knew, I was glad I hadn't gotten my wish. I would never have given myself a chance to know him otherwise, and I would have missed out on a wonderful man. I wouldn't have been able to handle the burden he carried long enough to get close to him. It hurt too much and it would have created a barrier between us.

"Savannah?" Rhys asked quietly.

"I'm okay," I replied, my voice hoarse. "I'm fine."

"Are you sure?"

"Yes, I'm sure." I rested my cheek on his shoulder, my forehead pressed into the curve of his neck, and tried to relax. In my mind, the remnants of his emotions swirled and I needed to get a handle on them.

I also needed to get a grip on myself because with a single glimpse into Rhys' heart, it was clear that I was falling in love with a complex and tortured man.

CHAPTER SEVENTEEN

Rhys

S OMETHING HAD CHANGED between Savannah and I since the night my amulet came off when she removed my shirt.

Her shyness hadn't disappeared completely, but it had lessened. She seemed more open and affectionate. She no longer hesitated to touch me or pull me in for a kiss when she wanted one. She didn't try to shield her thoughts and feelings from me, mentally or verbally. Savannah also spoke her mind more often. If there was something she wanted to know, she asked.

I felt as though she was offering me a gift. The gift of herself.

I wanted to take what she gave, but I held myself back. I knew that if I unleashed my desire completely that I would never be able to let her go, even if she wanted me to. Savannah Baker was the woman I loved and there would be no going back once I had her body.

This morning, when I dropped her off at *The Magic Bean*, she leaned over and kissed me before she got out of the car.

"I'll see you at three," she said as she opened the door. Before she climbed out, she looked over at me. "And I think it's time to revisit our discussion about hooking up as a part of dating."

I stared at her in shock as she grinned and shut the passenger door before hurrying inside the coffee shop. A few days ago,

Savannah never would have said something like that to me without turning a charming shade of pink. Today, there was an inviting gleam in her eye when she spoke the words.

She clearly intended to torture me. That was the only explanation.

Now it was two-thirty and I decided to go back to the shop in order to speak with Ava. I'd called Kerry earlier in the day and she hadn't been able to tell me anything more about Rhiannon, but she had given me the phone number of a witch in the U.K. that I hoped would be of some help.

When I entered *The Magic Bean*, Ava was behind the bar as usual, cleaning equipment. Savannah was nowhere to be found, but I noticed that the curtain to the reading room was closed and assumed that she was inside.

"Hi, Rhys," she greeted me.

As I drew closer, I saw signs of stress and worry on her face. It was clear that this situation with Rhiannon was wearing on her. Like me, she'd run into dead ends while looking for information on the witch. It was as if the woman had appeared out of thin air.

"Hi, Ava," I replied. I held out the piece of paper in my hand. "I spoke with my friend in Dallas and she gave me the number of a witch in the United Kingdom. I told Kerry that I thought it would be best if you called. It's been my experience that witches aren't overly fond of me."

Ava nodded and took the paper from me. "Thank you, Rhys. I'm getting truly pissed off about this entire situation. I still don't understand how a dark witch as powerful as Rhiannon escaped notice all these years."

I shrugged. "She may be very good at avoiding other witches."

Ava's expression grew thoughtful. "Maybe."

"Is Savannah giving a reading?" I asked.

Ava nodded. "It's for a woman who was recently widowed.

She's having a tough time," she answered, her eyes sad.

Without asking, she began to make me a glass of iced tea flavored with lemon and agave nectar. Summer had come to Austin, and I didn't want hot coffee in the middle of the afternoon.

"Thanks," I said when she placed the glass in front of me. Since Savannah and I had begun to spend so much time together, Ava refused to take my money when I came into the coffee shop. At first I tried to put extra money in the tip jar but it kept appearing back in my wallet, so I'd given up. The witch didn't want my money and no amount of pushing or sneaking would force her to change her mind.

I stood at the counter and talked with Ava as I waited for Savannah to finish her tarot reading. As soon as the curtain opened, I immediately noticed that Savannah looked drawn and pale. When our eyes met, she smiled tiredly, but shook her head. A woman emerged from the room, dabbing her eyes with a tissue. She spoke quietly with Savannah and then disappeared into the bathroom at the back of the store.

Savannah watched her client until the bathroom door shut, took a deep breath, and walked toward me. She was wearing one of the long flowing dresses she seemed to favor now that the weather had become hot. The straps were thin and bared her shoulders and part of her chest and back. She looked fresh and pretty even during the middle of a hot summer day "Hi, babe," she said, rising up on her toes to give me a light kiss on the lips.

I sensed the emotional exhaustion pulling at her limbs as soon as she touched me. The emotions of her client were weighing on her, dragging her down. I clasped her waist with my hands, wishing I could take some of the burden from her. I could see the strain it caused when she took on the feelings of another person.

No sooner did I have the thought when I felt a thread of energy from her. Slowly but surely, the grief and sorrow that had transferred from her client moved between us. Shocked, I released her waist and stepped back.

"What's wrong?" she asked, staring up at me with concern. "You just went pale."

I studied her face and realized that the color had returned to her cheeks. The faint lines around her eyes and on her forehead had disappeared.

"How do you feel?" I asked her, wondering if she even noticed the stream of energy and emotions that transferred between us.

She frowned slightly. "Weird. I feel better."

Ava cleared her throat behind us and offered two plastic cups of iced tea to Savannah. "Your client just came out of the bathroom. Give her one of these on the house and stop groping your boyfriend in the store." She grinned wickedly. "I've always wanted to say that to someone, but all my employees have been strangely well-behaved."

Savannah huffed and took the tea. "Rhys and I weren't even touching anymore."

"Doesn't matter," Ava argued. "I saw you kiss him. That's groping in my book."

Rolling her eyes with a laugh, Savannah took both glasses of tea and walked over to the woman who had exited the bathroom a few seconds ago. They talked for a few moments and Savannah handed her one of the cups and walked her toward the door. They went outside and I noticed that they both seemed lighter.

"What just happened?" Ava murmured behind me.

I faced her. "I'm not sure."

"I felt the magic, Rhys. What did you do?"

"I don't know, Ava," I shot back. "I was holding Savannah and I felt the grief and sorrow she'd absorbed from her client and I wanted to take it away. Then suddenly I felt those emotions transfer to me. It felt," I swallowed hard. "It felt like feeding."

My stomach twisted sickeningly. I never wanted to feed from someone I loved. It was dangerous and wrong.

Ava watched me carefully. "Did you see her face when she walked out a few seconds ago?"

"What do you mean?"

"She looked better after you touched her, as though some of the weight had been taken off her shoulders." The witch tilted her head to the side and narrowed her eyes. "It was as if you helped her by taking the emotions from her."

I shook my head. "It doesn't matter. I did it without her permission and I shouldn't have."

Ava made a humming sound in the back of her throat. "This could be good," she said, ignoring my statement. "I know how much her contact with other people weighs on her. She would never admit it but it exhausts her to go into public places. She's had to isolate herself so much over the last few years that I'm the only person she saw regularly. Now, there's you. And you might be able to help her deal with all of that."

"Ava, didn't you hear me? I took from her without her permission. It's wrong," I repeated.

Ava smacked her hand down on the counter. "Stop!" she exclaimed. "Yes, you should talk to her about it and definitely get her permission before you do it again, but you have to understand that *you can help her*, Rhys. You can make it possible for her to leave her house without passing out or go to a restaurant without having a meltdown."

Her words brought back the memory of the night I took Savannah to the Driskill Grill. She scared the hell out of me that evening.

"You can make her life better, Rhys. You already are just by being in it, but now you can help her reconnect with the rest of the world again."

The door to the shop opened and the bell rang, but this time the sound was different. Immediately, Ava stiffened, as though an alarm had gone off. I looked over my shoulder to see Rhiannon and Macgrath enter the store.

The witch looked pale and perfect, as though the hot summer sun didn't touch her when she was outside. Her vampire henchman seemed just as unaffected.

"Good afternoon," Ava said pleasantly. Her friendliness surprised me and I couldn't resist glancing at her. Her expression was neutral but her eyes glittered bright lavender. That was my only indication that she was disturbed by the dark witch's presence. Even her emotions seemed solid and calm.

"Hello, again, Ava," Rhiannon said, removing her dark sunglasses. Her dark eyes roamed over me. "Rhys."

"What can I get for you today?" Ava asked politely.

"I'll take an ice green tea. Unsweetened." Rhiannon answered.

While Ava made her drink, the vampire with her prowled around the shop, picking up items off shelves and replacing them exactly as he found them. I watched him with narrowed eyes. The implacable facade he presented last week had worn thin. Beneath the veneer I could see his frustration and agitation with Rhiannon. He didn't want to be here, but for some reason he felt obligated.

The door opened once again and Savannah entered. To her credit, she only hesitated a split second before she walked straight toward me with a cool smile pasted on her face.

Rhiannon looked at her. "Hello, Savannah."

"Rhiannon," she replied.

As soon as Savannah was within reach, I put my arm around her and drew her front against my side. I wanted her close in case things went badly.

Ava placed a large cup filled with ice and green tea in front of Rhiannon. "That will be three dollars," she stated.

Rhiannon lifted her brows in surprise. The last time she'd been in, Ava hadn't charged her for her coffee. Without a word, she reached into her purse and pulled out a twenty-dollar bill, handing it over to Ava.

"Keep the change. It's the least I can do."

"Thank you," Ava replied simply, refusing to rise to the bait.

"Have you given my offer any more thought?" Rhiannon asked her.

Ava shrugged. "Honestly, no. I wasn't interested in selling my property to you last week and I'm not interested this week either."

"What if I threw in an extra five hundred thousand dollar bonus?"

Ava shook her head. "Still not interested."

Macgrath appeared nearby. "So what does interest you?" he asked, his gaze intent on Ava's face.

She frowned at him for a moment. "What do you mean?"

"I'm wondering if anything interests you or if you're one of those witches that believes she above such trivial things."

Ava's face darkened with anger. "I do not believe myself above anyone. And I prefer to share my interests and pursuits with those I consider friends rather than perfect strangers," she retorted.

Savannah made a small sound in the back of her throat and tucked her face against my chest. Her body shook slightly and I realized she was trying to stifle laughter. I couldn't imagine what she found humorous about this situation, but I would definitely ask her when we were alone in her home.

Macgrath seemed completely unfazed by the putdown. "And what does one have to do to become your friend?"

The insinuation behind his question was clearly sexual and Ava's eyes sparked with blue and purple fire. "I'm not sure I care to share that with you."

The vampire smirked, clearly enjoying the exchange. "What

would you like to share with me?"

"Macgrath, I think that's enough for one day," Rhiannon re-monstrated. "We wouldn't want to upset Ms. Amaris too much and have her kick us out of her lovely shop."

The look the vampire shot her was full of venom and hatred, but he masked it before she saw. "Of course not."

Ava and I exchanged a glance and I knew she saw it too based on her facial expression.

"Perhaps I'll come visit you again, Savannah," Rhiannon stated. "And enjoy your lovely garden."

My muscles coiled at her statement and I felt Savannah tense at my side as well. Before either of us could react, Rhiannon replaced her sunglasses on her face and swayed out the door.

Without waiting a beat, Ava lifted a hand and snapped her fingers. The door locked and the sign flipped to show that the store was closed. With another wave of her hand, Ava lowered the shades over the door and windows so that no one could see in.

"I think we should have a talk and maybe call the witch in the United Kingdom," she stated.

"I agree."

"Wait, what witch in the United Kingdom?" Savannah asked.

"We'll meet at your house and talk about it. I don't want to have the discussion in the shop," Ava stated.

"Why not?"

"It's too easy to eavesdrop in a place like this. I can't put too many charms on the shop or the witches won't come in," Ava explained. "I have wards on all my rental homes to protect my tenants' privacy, so our conversation won't be overheard."

"We'll help you clean up and we'll all leave together."

Ava nodded. "Then let's not waste time."

Thirty minutes later, I parked my SUV in front of Savannah's house and we climbed out. As soon as Savannah unlocked the front door, Satchel came running up to us, mewing loudly.

Savannah bent down and picked her up, stroking her back. "Hi, kitty," she crooned.

Satchel butted her head against Savannah's chin, purring in contentment.

Ava followed us inside and shut the door. "I need a glass of wine," she stated, heading toward the kitchen. I could hear the clink of the glass as she pulled a bottle from the fridge. "You know what, I need two glasses. One for each hand."

Savannah watched her, her gaze contemplative. "You know, I've never seen her so off-balance," she murmured. "But I don't think it was Rhiannon who affected her like this."

I didn't either. The sparks flying between Ava and Macgrath had been so strong they were nearly visible. I also noticed that Rhiannon didn't like it much. In fact, she clearly despised Macgrath's open flirtation with Ava.

Ava returned to the living room, three wineglasses clutched by their stems in one hand, a bottle of wine under one arm, and another gripped in her other hand. "Now, we need to discuss a few things," she stated in a firm tone. She placed the wine bottles on the coffee table one by one, then set the glasses down and started filling them. When we didn't move quickly enough, she glanced up at us. "Come take a glass of wine so we can discuss this."

I shook my head. "None for me thanks." I didn't like the sweet wine that she and Savannah tended to drink.

"Then it's a good thing the third glass is already for me," she quipped.

Savannah chuckled, but there was tension in her voice. She moved over to the couch, settling on the cushions and taking the glass that Ava held out to her. I moved next to her, grunting as Satchel jumped from Savannah's lap to mine, landing directly on my crotch.

"First of all," Ava began, looking straight at Savannah, "Rhys will be staying with you from now until this situation is resolved."

To my surprise, Savannah nodded. "That sounds like a good idea."

Ava must have been surprised too because her eyes widened. "What?"

Savannah drank her wine. "Clearly Rhiannon's comment about coming to visit me was a threat and it's not as if Rhys isn't over here most of the time anyway."

Ava leaned back in the chair she settled in. "Well, that was easy." She finished off her first glass of wine and reached for the second. "Now, on to the next thing. Rhys accidentally siphoned some emotions from you today after your reading, Savannah. It was an accident."

I stared at her in shock and not a little anger. "Ava, I think maybe that's something I should talk to Savannah about alone."

Ava shook her head. "No, because you don't understand what happened and I do."

"How could I not understand what happened?" I asked her, my voice getting louder. "I fed from her! You and I both know it!" Savannah's cool hand rested on my shoulder, calming me slightly. I realized suddenly that she was drawing negative energy from me in an effort to make me feel better. I took her hand and held it between mine. "Please don't do that, Savannah."

"Do what?" she asked, frowning at me in confusion.

"I can feel you taking my emotions into yourself. You were trying to calm me, which I appreciate, but it's not necessary."

"I don't know what you're talking about, Rhys. I could tell by your behavior that you were upset and that was all."

"Then why do I feel calmer?" I asked her.

"Because you care for her," Ava interrupted. "That's what I was trying to tell you earlier. You balance each other out. When

Savannah is exposed to too many emotions and she's going into overload, you're able to take some of that weight from her. It provides you with nourishment and feeds you when you need it. You fit together."

I glanced at Savannah and she shrugged at me as if she didn't know what else to say.

"How is that possible, Ava?" Savannah asked. "There's a difference between emotions and someone's soul. How does that even work?"

"Emotions are part of the soul, Savannah," Ava replied. "They're all connected. You can't have one without the other. You can't always control the amount of emotions you take in, but he can act as your release valve."

"Look, maybe we should talk about this another time," I suggested. "We have larger concerns right now."

Ava nodded, but she didn't look happy. "We do, but we can't call the witch in the U.K. until tomorrow morning. It's probably close to the middle of the night there."

I didn't like it, but she was right. "Tomorrow."

Ava stood. "Now, I need to go home and see if I can find a hex that will turn a vampire into a toad," she stated.

"Are you okay to drive?" Savannah asked.

"I'm fine," Ava reassured her. "I have a potion I can take."

Savannah stood up and gave Ava a hug. "We'll talk tomorrow, okay? Are you opening the shop?"

Ava sighed. "I don't know. I don't want to, but at the same time, if Rhiannon is watching, I don't want her to think she has us running scared. Plus, I don't know how long this is going to go on and I can't afford to close it for a prolonged period of time."

I got up, followed Ava to the door, and walked her out to her car. After she climbed inside behind the driver's seat, I bent down to speak to her. "Please call me tomorrow after you speak to the witch."

Ava nodded. "I will."

"And call one of us when you get home."

She opened her mouth to argue but I shook my head. "Just because Rhiannon focused on Savannah doesn't mean that she won't come after you too."

Ava sighed. "You're right. I'll call you when I get home." She reached into her purse and pulled out a small vial. After she opened it, she tipped it back and drained it in one swallow. Making a face, she said, "Yuck. It works so well but I can never seem to make it taste better no matter what I do."

I laughed and straightened, closing the car door. Ava started the vehicle and backed out of the driveway. I waited until she was out of sight before I walked up the steps to the porch. Savannah stood outside with her arms crossed over her chest, a strange expression on her face.

"You should probably go pack some clothes since you might be staying with me for a while."

CHAPTER EIGHTEEN

Savannah

I STARED AT the dark ceiling of my bedroom, wondering if Rhys was asleep yet. Glancing over at the clock, I saw that it was just after midnight and sighed. When Ava suggested that he spend the night, I wasn't sure what I expected, but it definitely wasn't him insisting that he sleep in the guest room.

I turned over in the bed and stared at the wall, watching the shadow of the tree outside my window sway as the wind blew. I knew what I wanted, but I was too intimidated to ask for it. For so many years, I'd been alone and now it felt strange for me to tell a man that I wanted to have sex with him.

But I did. I'd even added a box of condoms to my grocery delivery list and I'd been unable to look the delivery driver in the eye when I accepted my bags.

I wanted Rhys, body and soul.

If I wanted him, I would have to go and get him. Rhys was not a modern man who expected a woman to be intimate with him. Chastity was valued during his time as a human and it was only in the last few centuries that attitudes had loosened somewhat.

I got out of bed and looked down at the pretty purple night-gown edged with black lace I wore. I'd put it on in the hopes that Rhys would come to my room when we went to bed. Hopes that remained unfulfilled.

If he wouldn't come to me, I would go to him.

I opened the nightstand drawer next to my bed and removed a condom from the box I'd opened earlier. I tucked it into the material that stretched over my breast. Satchel opened one eye and watched me as I crept around the end of my bed and toward the door, but she didn't move. Hoping that she would stay in my bedroom, I walked down the hall toward the guest room, surprised to see the door standing open.

I hesitated in the hall, right outside his door, my courage wavering.

"Savannah?" Rhys called quietly. "Are you okay?"

Taking a deep breath, I reminded myself that I was asking for what I wanted. I walked around the corner. Rhys hadn't bothered to close the curtains over the blinds and the moonlight poured in, falling across the bed in thin lines. His upper body was bare and the lean muscles of his shoulders and chest were illuminated in the pale beams.

My mouth was suddenly dry and I swallowed hard at the sight. He was beautiful. "I, um, couldn't sleep," I murmured, standing just inside the door to the guest room, staring at him like some sort of creeper.

He sat up, leaning back against the headboard. "What's wrong?"

Unable to stop myself, I took several more steps into the room and heard his quick intake of breath when the moonlight touched my body. "There's something I need but I'm afraid to ask for it," I replied, my voice barely above a whisper.

"I told you that you could ask me anything and I meant it."

I crept forward, putting one hand on the end of the bed then lifting a knee and crawling up the mattress toward him. I heard his muted groan as I moved closer.

"Savannah, I'm not sure—"

I stopped with my knees on each side of his thighs and straightened so my bottom rested on his legs. "Do you want me, Rhys?" I asked, unsure of what I would do if he said no.

"Of course I do," he replied gruffly. "But I'm not certain you understand what you're doing."

I frowned down at him. "I'm nearly twenty-nine years old, Rhys. I realize I've not had thousands of years under my belt, but I am an adult and I know what I want." I started to shift off the bed, hurt welling within me.

His hands shot out and gripped my wrists. "That's not what I mean," he said, holding me still. I stared at the amulet that rested against his sternum, unable to meet his eyes. "Look at me, Savannah," he pleaded.

Feeling exposed, I lifted my gaze to his face and felt my heart thump hard in my chest at the sight. His eyes were fierce and his jaw was clenched tightly, as though he were holding himself back with iron control.

"I want you more than anything, but I need you to understand what this means to me. If you let me touch you like this, I won't be able to let you go. I will be yours forever."

My body began to tremble as he spoke. I craved what he was offering me. A partner who would never want to leave me despite my abilities. I was falling in love with him and I knew that his feelings for me were strong. He was everything I wanted in a partner, even though I hadn't realized it before.

"I like the idea of you belonging to me forever," I replied.

His hold on my wrists tightened. Then he pulled me forward until my knees straddled his hips and he placed my palms on his chest. I could feel the hard, fast rhythm of his heart and knew that he was just as affected as I was.

"Then touch me," he whispered.

I splayed my fingers wide, feeling the firm muscle beneath his hot skin. I shifted my body against his and he made a low noise in his throat. Moving my hands down his chest, my fingertips trailed over his nipples and down his abdomen. His muscles twitched under my touch and his hands came up to grab my hips, pulling me tightly against him.

Through the thin blanket and sheets between us, I felt the hard ridge of his erection grind against me. I gasped, undulating against him once again. I wanted to feel more.

I cried out as he reared up and flipped us over on the bed, coming down on his knees between my spread thighs. The blankets were tangled around our legs, holding me prisoner beneath him, but I didn't care. I didn't want to escape him.

I realized he wore nothing beneath the blankets but a pair of silky athletic shorts. The material slid against my inner thighs, making my skin tingle. My palms were still on Rhys' chest and trapped between our bodies.

He looked down at me, his blue eyes glittering in the moonlight. Slowly, he lowered his head and took my mouth with his. I tugged my arms free of his weight and arched beneath him, pressing my breasts against his chest. The heat of his skin burned through the silk of my nightgown. I could feel the cool metal and stone of his amulet where it rested against my breastbone.

Wrapping my arms around him, I gave myself over to the kiss, my tongue dancing with his and my legs circling his hips to bring him closer. Rhys groaned into my mouth, giving me more of his weight.

I felt his hard length at the juncture of my thighs and moved restlessly beneath him. I wanted skin-to-skin contact, to feel his naked body against mine. Instead of telling him what I wanted, I unwound my arms from around his shoulders and tugged the straps of my nightgown down over my arms. The condom wrapper scraped my skin as I slid down the top of the garment. I pulled it loose from the fabric and set it on the pillow next to my head.

Rhys lifted his mouth from mine, raising his upper body so he could see me. Resting his weight on one arm, he traced a finger over my collarbone and down to my bared breasts.

"You're beautiful," he murmured, his eyes taking in my partially clothed body.

My nipples beaded as he drew light circles around each one with his fingertip. Then his mouth closed over the sensitive tip, enveloping my nipple in wet heat. I couldn't breathe as the sensation overwhelmed me. After so many years without a man's touch, the contact was intense.

When his tongue flicked my nipple, my back arched and I cried out. My body melted into the bed when his mouth moved to my other breast, giving it the same treatment. He levered his weight off me, lifting his hips so he could push the nightgown down my body. I took advantage of his position and hooked my fingers in the waistband of his shorts. Within seconds, he was naked and all I wore were a pair of pink lace panties.

He brought his weight back down on top of me and our mouths met again in a kiss full of desperation and uncontrolled desire. I was ready for him. Ready for everything he offered me.

Lifting my hips, I pulled the lace panties down, pushing them to my knees and struggling to free my legs. Rhys reached down and yanked them off, leaving me bare. His hand traveled back up my leg until he reached my center. I spread my thighs wider as first one finger then another slid inside of me. His touch was incredible after the years of loneliness and emptiness.

I felt the release already building inside me, the ache between my legs turning into a burn.

"Rhys, I need you," I whispered. I felt the tip of his cock brush my center and lifted a hand to his chest. "Wait, wait, we need a condom."

I reached up and found the packet, tearing it open. When I tried to hand the condom to him, he looked at me in confusion. "What is that?" he asked.

I realized then just how long it had been since he'd been with anyone. He didn't understand about contraception. "It's a condom. It prevents pregnancy and the spread of diseases," I answered.

"Will it hurt?"

"No, it won't hurt," I explained. "It's what we call a contraceptive. I'm not on the pill that prevents pregnancy and I'm not ready to be a mom just yet, so we won't be able to make love without it."

He stared into my eyes and nodded. "Okay, show me how to use it."

With shaking hands, I reached between us and placed the condom at the head of his erection. He let out a harsh breath as I rolled it down his length, his eyes watching every motion of my hands.

When I was done, I wrapped my fingers around him, guiding him inside me. His eyes met mine and one of his hands slid beneath me to cup the back of my neck. I sucked in a deep breath as he slipped inside me a little at a time. His other hand rested on my hip, pinning me to the bed as I trembled against him.

"Am I hurting you?" he asked.

"No," I answered, trying to breathe through the pressure. After seven years, my body struggled to accept him inside me. "Just…go slowly please."

He nodded, leaning down to brush his lips against mine in a gentle kiss. As he kissed me, he withdrew slightly and pushed forward again. He moved an inch at a time until finally he was seated deep inside my body.

I was nearly wild with need by the time he fully entered me, desperate for him to move, to set a rhythm that would take me over the edge where I was poised. I kissed him fiercely then, nipping his bottom lip.

He made a sound low in his throat and his body grew taut. "Savannah," he whispered. "I don't want to hurt you."

"I'm ready," I insisted, lifting my hips toward his, using my body to urge him on.

He withdrew from me and thrust forward slowly. With each movement, my body followed his, seeking a deeper contact. Craving it with every fiber of my being.

My hands clutched at his back and buttocks, pulling him toward me each time he slid outward. "Faster. Please," I gasped, my muscles twitching with the orgasm that swelled within me. I needed more to carry me to the pinnacle.

Finally, he gave me what I needed. My thighs tightened around his hips and I rocked against him, a long moan slipping from my throat.

Within moments, I was there, hovering on the brink. Rhys lowered his head and pulled my nipple into his mouth as he moved and that was all it took.

Crying out, I fisted my hands in his hair and went flying. The spasms seemed to go on and on, shaking my body to the core. Rhys' mouth crashed into mine, our tongues tangling, as he kept moving, drawing out the orgasm until it nearly hurt.

I whimpered against his lips and he groaned, thrusting into me one last time as his body went rigid. After a long moment, he relaxed against me, letting his weight pin me to the bed. I relished his warmth as my body quaked with intermittent aftershocks. Tucking my face into his neck, I kissed his throat and collarbone, my tongue darting out to taste his skin.

As our breathing returned to normal, Rhys lifted his head and looked down at me, his eyes concerned. "Did I hurt you?" he asked.

"No, that was perfect," I sighed.

The corner of his mouth lifted in a small, crooked smile. "Perfect?"

I snuggled into him, wondering how I had waited so long to seduce him. He felt incredible. "Definitely."

Moving carefully, he pulled out of my body and looked down. "What am I supposed to do with this now?" he asked.

I followed the direction of his gaze and saw the condom. "I'll throw it away," I volunteered.

Rhys shook his head. "No, you stay here. I'll take care of it."

He climbed out of the bed and I watched as he walked out of the room. Even in the watery moonlight, I could see the beautiful musculature of his back and buttocks and enjoyed the loose-hipped grace of his stride. While he was gone, I took a moment to straighten the blankets and sheets on the bed, locate my panties and slip them on. I briefly debated putting on my nightgown but decided against it. I wanted to enjoy the feeling of Rhys' skin against mine.

Stretching out in the bed, I pulled the sheets up to my chest. Now that Rhys was no longer next to me, the room felt cool. He returned a few moments later with a glass of water in his hand. Considering how my mouth went dry when I got my first true glimpse of Rhys' naked body from the front, I needed the liquid he offered to me.

"Thanks," I murmured, taking the glass from him. Unbidden, my eyes wandered over his body as I drank. He reminded me of a Greek or Roman statue and he seemed completely at ease with his nudity. When I finally met his eyes, I felt a blush heat my face because he was watching me with a small smirk on his lips.

"Seen enough?" he asked, gently teasing.

"For now," I replied, feeling surprisingly bold.

He grinned wide enough to reveal those intriguing creases in his cheeks that weren't quite dimples, but were charming just the same. He took the glass when I held it out and drained the rest of the water from it before setting it on the dresser and coming back over to the bed.

He climbed beneath the covers and pulled me against his side so that my cheek rested on his shoulder.

"How do you feel?" I asked him, suddenly wondering if his emotions resembled mine at all.

"Happy," he sighed. "How do you feel?" he asked in return.

I tilted my head back to look at him. "You can't tell."

"Maybe," he drawled.

I smiled at him. "I feel the same way you do. Happy."

And in love, but I didn't say it aloud. I needed a little more time to come to terms with that feeling before I shared it with him. I might have loved some of the men in my past, but I had never felt like this before.

When Rhys cuddled me tighter against his side, I had an inkling that he already knew anyway but he was willing to wait until I was ready to say it.

I laid my hand on his chest, stroking his skin idly as I drifted closer to sleep. I decided that I wanted to sleep like this every night for the rest of my life.

CHAPTER NINETEEN

Rhys

I WOKE UP to an empty bed and very nearly panicked. For a moment, I thought that perhaps Savannah had been taken. Then I heard the sound of the shower running in Savannah's room. I rolled out of bed and walked naked through the house. I felt the sudden urge to bathe. Or at least stand in the shower and watch Savannah wash her body. A body that I had touched and kissed last night. I'd fallen asleep holding her, feeling more at peace than I had in my long life.

Satchel sat in front of the open bathroom door, her eyes narrowed on me as her tail twitched with irritation.

"Sorry, kitty, but you should know my heart belonged to your owner before I even met you."

She turned her nose up at me and pranced out of the bedroom with her head held high. I bit back a laugh at the cat's attitude. I'd never met another animal with such a noticeable personality. It was almost as if the cat had a human brain.

I walked into the bathroom, my eyes immediately drawn to the glass shower stall in the corner. Steam wafted in the air and I could hear Savannah humming softly as the water washed over her. Silently, I opened the door to the shower and stood completely still. Last night, I'd seen her body in the dim light of the moon, but now the sight of her hit me in the gut. She was gorgeous. Her pale, freckled skin was pink from the hot water and the slope of her back narrowed at her waist before flaring out into amply curved hips and buttocks.

Her hands were massaging shampoo into her scalp and she suddenly turned toward me and tilted her head back, her eyes closed. Soap washed down her body, sliding over her breasts and stomach to the apex of her thighs.

My body responded to the sight, my shaft growing hard. I stepped into the shower and shut the door behind me. It clicked and Savannah's head turned toward me and she opened her eyes.

"Oh, my God, Rhys. You scared me!" she gasped, pressing a hand to her chest.

"I'm sorry," I apologized, stepping into her space and crowding her body with mine.

When my cock brushed her stomach, she looked down and her eyes widened. Before she could speak, I clamped my hands around her waist and lifted her off her feet. Savannah yelped but wrapped her legs around my hips and her arms around my shoulders, surrounding me with her limbs.

"Rhys?" My name was a question.

My only answer was to kiss her. I found that I wanted her even more now in the light of day than I had last night after centuries of celibacy. Now that I knew how her skin tasted and how she sounded when she climaxed. How her body felt when it accepted mine deep inside.

I wanted to experience it again and again until I had memorized everything about her.

Savannah moaned and moved against me, the wet skin of her breasts rubbing my chest and her hot center pressed against my aching shaft. I was tempted to slide inside her then and there but remembered our conversation the night before.

Lifting my mouth from hers, I asked, "Do we need one of those condoms?"

She stared at me blankly for a moment then her eyes focused. "Yes. Yes, we do."

I let her slide down my body and she reached out to turn off the water as I opened the shower door and reached for a towel. I swiped some of the water from my body and hers but our skin was still damp when we stumbled into the bedroom and fell onto her bed.

Savannah put her hands on my shoulders, pushing me over onto my back. Climbing astride me, she reached over to the nightstand and removed a shiny black package from the drawer. Her breasts were level with my face, so I took advantage of our position and sucked her nipple into my mouth.

She arched into me, one of her hands grasping my hair as I laved her flesh with my tongue. I moved to her other breast and relished the sounds that escaped her throat.

Savannah shifted her hips and reached between us, her fingers curling around my cock. She stroked me firmly several times and I jerked against her. Though I'd just had her last night, it wasn't enough to satisfy years of hunger and desire for the touch of another.

I reached down and grasped her wrist, pulling her hand away from my body.

"Why'd you stop me?" she asked, her body shifting against mine.

I kissed her and nipped her bottom lip before lowering my mouth to her neck. I held her hand behind her back, using it to leverage her body closer. "You can touch me later," I murmured.

She struggled briefly until my mouth returned to her breasts, then she moaned.

"Are you wet for me?" I asked as I released her wrist and

reached between us to slide a finger over her center.

"Yes," she whispered, her hips rocking against my touch. Savannah straightened and ripped open the packet in her hand. "I don't want to wait any longer."

She moved back and put her hands on my shaft, rolling the condom over me. Though I understood the concept, I enjoyed watching her do it.

Once the condom was in place, she moved over me and guided me inside her body. I watched her move over me, a flush spreading from her breasts up to her neck. Her body was so tight and hot around me that it took all of my self-control to let her set the pace rather than slam into her over and over until we both came.

Savannah braced her hands on my chest as her hips rose and fell. I tugged at her nipples and felt her tighten around me with each pull. Her head fell back as she moved faster and ground her body against me. I knew she was close to her peak and I fisted her hair, pulling her torso down to use my mouth on her nipples.

Suddenly, she tensed over me, her body shaking wildly as she cried out, and I could no longer hold myself back. Twisting, I rolled our bodies and began to ride her hard, sliding deeper with each stroke.

She whimpered beneath me as she continued to climax and I was lost. I kissed her deeply as I emptied myself into her, swallowing every sound she made.

The frantic movements of our bodies eased until I thrust slowly in and out of her, enjoying the small spasms of her muscles around me.

"You make me forget myself," I murmured to her, sliding my lips across hers.

"What do you mean?" she asked, her question soft and slightly slurred.

"I want to take my time with you and enjoy your body, not fall on you like a rutting beast."

The haze over her dark eyes cleared and they sparkled up at me. "Fall on me like a rutting beast?" she repeated, her mouth curving.

I kissed her again, this time longer and harder than before. "What else would you call it?"

Her smile widened. "Uncontrollable passion?"

"Hmm. That sounds better, but I still want to taste every part of you." When Savannah shivered beneath me, it was my turn to smile. "I think you like that idea."

Her cheeks turned pink but she met my eyes. "I do, but only if I can return the favor." As she spoke, her hand smoothed over my back as though she were relishing the texture of my skin. "I think you're beautiful."

"So are you," I replied. I withdrew from her body slowly, hating that I needed to leave her, but the condom felt odd. "I'll be right back."

I walked into the bathroom, dropped the strange glove into the trashcan, and washed my hands. I disliked the condoms, but Savannah seemed adamant that she wasn't ready to have a child. I wasn't sure I could even father a babe, but I would wear whatever she asked me to if it meant I could have her.

When I returned to the bedroom, I found Savannah tucked beneath the covers, already asleep. Moving carefully, I climbed in beside her and curved my body around her back. Immediately, she snuggled back against me and sighed in her sleep.

Content, I slid one arm beneath her pillow and wrapped the other around her waist. I fell asleep holding the woman I loved and never once thought of the nightmares that had plagued me for weeks until last night.

CHAPTER TWENTY

Savannah

B EFORE I EVEN opened my eyes, I felt happy. Last night and this morning with Rhys had been everything that I hoped it would be. He touched me with reverence and passion, bringing my body to life in ways I'd never experienced before.

With my abilities, sex wasn't easy. While I was in high school and college, it saved me from making the mistake of having sex with boys who were only interested in sleeping with as many girls as they could. Then I met Neil, and he had loved me the way I thought I wanted to be loved. I discovered that I enjoyed sex. When Neil made love to me, he made sure I climaxed each time.

But last night had transcended every single one of those experiences even though foreplay had practically been an afterthought. Each time we made love, I felt the bond between us growing, almost as though it were a tangible connection that would eventually become visible.

I lay in the circle of Rhys' arms for a few moments, luxuriating in this warmth and the weight of his body. Finally, I had to get up. I needed to pee and my stomach was rumbling with hunger.

Carefully, I moved to the edge of the bed, got up, and crept into the bathroom. After I took care of business and washed my hands, I pulled a baggy t-shirt over my head and slipped on a pair of panties and cotton shorts.

Rhys was still sleeping peacefully as I came out of the bathroom and Satchel peered at me from behind his back, her gaze sleepy. Her possessiveness of my boyfriend aside, I was glad that my cat liked Rhys and he liked her. She might be just a pet to some people, but for many years she'd been my only constant companion against the loneliness.

I walked down the hall and straight into the kitchen. I prepped the coffee pot last night and it was full, but the contents were stone cold. With a sigh, I poured a mug full and stuck it in the microwave. Then I poured out the rest, washed the carafe, and set about making another pot.

As I drank my first cup of coffee, I carried it out on the deck behind the house and stared out into my backyard. My mind wandered to Rhys. While I wanted to sit and moon over him, I also needed to think. Yesterday, Ava said he had taken the excess of emotions from me and, when I thought about it, I could pinpoint the exact moment. I felt…lighter when he did it.

I knew that Rhys loathed that part of himself. He felt it was parasitic, the feeding on the emotions of others. Unlike vampires, who could often find partners who would freely give them what they needed, he was in an untenable position. If too many beings learned of his existence, he would be hunted down by supernatural creatures of all types. He couldn't tell anyone what he needed to survive, his only option was to take it.

Also, the fact that he hadn't wanted to be what he was, but rather made against his will, affected his view of his need to feed. Vampires and shifters alike were often born or they asked to be turned. Because Gaius made him without his compliance, he saw himself as a monster.

I knew the only thing that would change his view would be him. He needed to open his mind, to accept that he wasn't evil. All

I could do was love him and accept him as he was.

There was one way to help him, but I was certain he would balk at the idea. I hoped that he would at least listen to what I had to say because not only would it help him, it would help me as well.

I heard the door open behind me and turned in time to see Rhys stepping outside, wearing nothing but the athletic shorts he'd worn to bed the night before.

In the bright light of day, his body was mesmerizing. I couldn't tear my eyes away until I heard him chuckle.

"You're good for my ego," he said, walking over to the lounge chair next to mine. He sat down and I realized he was holding a cup of coffee in his hand.

"You know you're hot," I replied primly, sipping my own coffee.

"Until I met you, very few people felt true attraction toward me."

"*That* I don't believe," I argued. "Women fawn over you every time you come into the shop."

He smiled, but it didn't reach his eyes. "There's a difference between admiring the physical aspects of a person and being attracted to them on a deeper level."

I couldn't disagree with that because I'd witnessed it many times personally. "Good point," I mumbled.

As we drank our coffee in the late morning sun, I leaned back on the lounge chair and searched for the words I needed to say.

"Rhys, I want to talk to you about something," I stated.

I could feel the tension emanating from his body as soon as I said the words, but he didn't reply.

"It's about something Ava said yesterday." His tension level rose again, but I continued anyway. "She talked about how you could help me deal with all the excess emotions that build up when

I'm around other people and," I swallowed hard, because even though his amulet made it impossible for me to get a strong read on his emotions, I could still feel the echoes. He didn't want me to say what I was about to say. "I think I want to try."

I knew before I looked over at him that he was shaking his head. "Savannah, I think that's a bad idea."

"Rhys, please just hear me out."

I could tell he wanted to get up and walk away, it was in every line of his body, but I was certain that we needed to do this. For both of us.

"If I can give you what you need and do so willingly, why shouldn't I?" I asked. "You would also be helping me. I'm tired of living my life only here in my home or inside the Bean. I want to be able to go out to dinner, or to the movies, or on vacation. I'm living a narrow life right now, and if this works, you will be giving me something I want very much."

Rhys stared at me, his indecision written clearly in his expression. "Savannah," he began.

I knew he was going to say no without even thinking about what I was asking or what I wanted. "Rhys, please," I pleaded. "I fully understand what you will be doing and I'm *still* asking you to do it. Not even asking, begging. Yesterday, after Mary left the shop, my head ached from her pain and sorrow. All I wanted to do was curl up into a ball and hide in a dark room. After you took that from me, I felt better, more like myself. My head no longer hurt and neither did my heart. You took it away." I had to stop and clear my throat before I continued. It felt tight with the emotions rising within me. "I have no choice but to take on the pain of others. I can't stop it completely. I might be able to block some of it out, but not all. There is no spell or magic that can help me the way your amulet helps you. Nothing except your abilities."

I could tell I was getting through to him. He no longer looked as though he were shutting down, so I pushed a little harder.

"I don't want to live half of a life with you, Rhys. I want to go places with you, experience things. And, someday, we might have children who share your abilities. How will they survive? Will you call them monsters?"

He looked taken aback by my questions. "Of course not. Children are not monstrous."

"But they could be like you," I pointed out. "And you say you're a monster."

Rhys stared at me. I couldn't feel his emotions, but I could plainly see that he was torn.

"I just want you to think about it," I said softly. "I want you to see yourself the way I see you, but I can't force you to change your mind."

His chin jerked as he absorbed what I said.

"Are you hungry?" I asked, changing the subject. "I was just thinking about what to make for breakfast. Well, technically I guess it would be lunch."

"No, I'm not hungry, but I can go pick up something for you to eat if you'd like."

I shook my head. "I'll just make some eggs and toast." I got to my feet and leaned over to kiss his cheek. "Do you want more coffee?"

He shook his head, his gaze unfocused as he looked out into the backyard. I knew he was thinking about everything I'd just said, but I didn't want to continue to push him. He needed time to digest it all and he wouldn't be able to do that if I kept talking about it.

With a heavy heart, I went back inside the house and set about making breakfast. The longer that Rhys sat on the deck, the more I began to question if I'd done the right thing. We'd only just made love for the first time last night and our relationship was still so new, even if it didn't feel that way.

He said that he would never let me go, but that was before I pushed him to do something he wasn't comfortable with. I couldn't help but wonder if it was a mistake to bring it up so soon. Maybe he wasn't as invested in me as I was in him. He'd been alone for so long, unused to compromising. Had I pushed him away with my request?

Doubts clouded my mind as I buttered toast and put scrambled eggs on my plate. My appetite had completely disappeared. Just as I was about to go back outside and tell Rhys not to worry about it, to forget everything I'd just said, the back door opened.

I looked at him, my heart in my throat, waiting for him to tell me that he couldn't do this, or that I was asking for too much from him. Instead, he looked lighter somehow, as though he'd shrugged off some of the weight that he carried on his shoulders.

"You're right," he murmured. "Any children we have wouldn't be monsters. I'm not sure if I will ever be able to see myself as you do, but even I can see that any child we create wouldn't be evil."

My legs nearly gave out beneath me when he spoke because that wasn't what I expected.

"I'm willing to try feeding from you because I want to give you the life that you long for. I didn't realize how trapped you are by your abilities and I don't want you to feel that way."

I smiled tremulously at him, relief filling me. "Thank you," I murmured. "I was freaking out, thinking that I pushed you too hard, too fast, and you would decide I wasn't worth the trouble. I've been sitting in here, thinking that I'd made a mistake."

Rhys frowned and came over to me, taking me by the arms. "I don't ever want you to question what I feel for you, Savannah." He slid his hands down to mine, lifted them to his chest, and placed them on his heart. "This heart belongs to you. It beats for you. I never want you to feel as though you have to hide how you feel from me. You told me the truth and it will take more than that for you to turn me away."

It seemed that Rhys wasn't the only person who needed to adjust their thinking. I also didn't know how to handle the fact that he'd talked about his feelings toward me several times and each time he implied that he loved me. We had only known each other for a handful of weeks, but I was already head over heels in love with him. It also seemed that he felt the same, but he hadn't said the words.

This morning, as we made love, they'd hovered on the tip of my tongue and I'd nearly spoken them aloud, but fear held me back. Fear of sharing too much, too soon.

I wanted to say them now, to share my thoughts and feelings with him so he understood that he had my heart as well.

Before I could speak, his cell phone buzzed on the counter. He glanced down and his body went still.

"It's Ava," he murmured. "She was supposed to call the witch in the U.K. this morning."

I stepped back and dropped my hands. "Do you mind putting it on speaker so I can hear what she has to say?"

Rhys nodded and picked up the phone. A few seconds later, Ava's voice came through the speaker. "Hey, Rhys. I waited a few hours because I thought you guys might want to sleep in this morning."

I choked back a laugh.

"Oh, hey, Savannah. How are you this beautiful summer morning?" she asked.

I felt my cheeks heat at her words because it was clear that she predicted what would happen last night. "I'm great."

"Hmmm. I think we should talk more about your answer later, but right now I have some important stuff to tell you about our mutual frenemy, Rhiannon. Apparently, she's been around as long as Rhys and she likes to cause trouble. The only reason we haven't heard of her before now is because she always gets someone else to do her dirty work, mainly a vampire named Macgrath. Margaret, that's the British witch that Kerry told us about, said that it's surprising she came to us herself. Her usual M.O. is to send Macgrath or another intermediary and never show her face."

I felt a cold finger of dread drag along my spine as Ava spoke.

"How is she trouble?" Rhys asked.

"She shows up and people disappear. Usually they're creatures with unique or strong powers. Witches, vampires, and shifters who are special or unusual in some way vanish not long after they meet with her intermediary or Macgrath. She also buys a lot of property and it's usually associated with a place of magical power, sacred places." Ava sighed. "I hate to say it but it sounds like she's a power whore to me. She's extremely strong and I think that her activities have something to do with that. It also means she's probably after you, Rhys. The legends about *animavores* hint that if your soul can be consumed so can your ability to siphon the souls of others. The soul of a supernatural being carries their essence, their power, which means she can then gather even more power."

I glanced at Rhys and saw how pale his face had become. "Essentially she intends to do what Cornelius did," he murmured. "She's going to build her power base to the point that she's unstoppable."

"Maybe," Ava replied. "I agree that she wants to build her power base, but she doesn't strike me as someone who wants to rule as a god. Her agenda seems to be strength and wealth. Everything she does makes her richer and more powerful, yet she doesn't show her face. She doesn't have the ego of a despot. If she did, she wouldn't rely mostly on her minions to do her dirty work. She would want people to recognize her and fear her. I think she has different motives for gaining power."

"I think you're right," I interjected. "Her goal is to be stronger but she doesn't want to be worshipped. She wants to be acknowledged and loved, but not by an entire population. She only wants the adulation of a certain person or persons. I could feel it when she was at the store. She's angry and she's hurt and she's allowed those feelings to fester for hundreds, if not thousands of years."

"Great," Ava replied. "We have a witch with anger management issues and a craving for power watching our every move. Nothing to worry about."

"At least we have a better understanding of what she wants," I stated. "If we understand what she wants, then we can find a way to deal with her."

Ava sighed. "I miss the old days when we could take care of a witch by binding her when she misbehaved. Now you have to provide proof and ask special permission from the council of high priests and priestesses."

"We'll deal with her," I said. "Together."

"All right, well Margaret gave me some ideas of where to look if I wanted to know more about Rhiannon. Including the old myths because apparently the woman has been around long enough that they're probably about her," Ava stated. "Rhys, please thank Kerry for her help with this."

"I will," Rhys agreed. "Surely there is something else we can do to help."

"There is, but I need more information before we discuss it. I'll be in touch," she promised.

"Bye, Ava," I said.

"In the meantime, enjoy yourselves." She gave a wicked laugh and hung up.

My face hot, I looked up at Rhys. His pensive expression made me forget my embarrassment at Ava's innuendo. "Hey, are you okay?"

He nodded. "I'm fine."

I gestured to the pan of eggs that I'd made that were likely cold now. "Are you sure you don't want some breakfast?"

"Actually, I think I do," he replied.

As I put the eggs on plates and warmed them up, I tried not to worry about what the future might bring and enjoy the moment.

When the time came, I would be glad that I did.

CHAPTER TWENTY-ONE

Rhys

S AVANNAH INSISTED ON going to *The Magic Bean* when she
discovered that Ava opened the store after all. When we
arrived, I had the opportunity to see a different side of Savannah.

She marched into the shop and right up to Ava. Then she lost
her temper.

"What were you thinking, coming here alone? I told you that I
wanted to be here when you had the store open and you ignored
me! I realize that you're a powerful witch in your own right, but
you are not invincible. If Rhiannon hunts supernatural creatures
with enormous talent, you are in danger too. What in the hell were
you thinking?"

I'd never seen Savannah angry before but I found that I enjoyed the sight. Her cheeks were flushed and her dark eyes were
bright. She looked vibrant and energy seemed to crackle around
her.

Ava looked toward me as though she were seeking my aid. I
crossed my arms over my chest and shook my head. There was no
way I was getting involved in this.

"Savannah, there are wards on the shop, I'm just as safe here as
I am at home," Ava said, trying to soothe her.

"Maybe, but what about your car? It's not as if it's a tank!"

Savannah put her hands on her hips. "You should move in with me until all this is over. We'll be safer all together."

Ava's eyes widened and moved to me again. This time I did intervene because it was clear that the witch didn't want to move in with us and I agreed that it was best if she didn't. Now that I'd enjoyed Savannah's body, I fully intended to do so on a regular basis. Having a houseguest would make that difficult.

"Savannah, you know that Ava can take care of herself," I pointed out.

Savannah turned toward me and I saw the sparkle of tears on her lower lashes. "I know she can take care of herself, Rhys, but she's one of the few people in this world I love and I want to know she's safe."

"What if I moved into Rhys' house?" Ava offered, her voice nearly desperate. I realized that the sight of Savannah's tears affected her deeply. "I would be close and we could ride to work together. He's staying with you so he won't need it." She looked toward me, her eyes begging me to agree.

"I think that's a good plan," I agreed.

Savannah narrowed her gaze and looked first at Ava then at me. "I guess that would work," she relented before turning back toward Ava. "But don't you ever do this again. Until things are settled or you find someone to help you, you don't come in and open the shop alone."

It was the first time I'd seen Ava look the least bit cowed. She nodded silently.

"Fine, then we should get to work," Savannah said smartly, walking behind the counter and stowing her purse beneath it.

As Savannah gathered her apron and pulled it over her head, Ava looked at me and I bit back a smile.

"I've never seen her so angry," Ava murmured.

"Really?" I asked. "I thought you two had known each other

for ten years or so."

"We have," she admitted. "But I've never seen Savannah truly angry. She gets frustrated, disappointed, hurt, and sad, but never angry. It was a little scary."

I couldn't hold back the chuckle that built up in my chest. "She loves you."

"I know," Ava replied with a sigh. "And I love her." She glanced at me, a smile playing at the corners of her mouth. "Speaking of love, you two look all loved up."

I shook my head at her and didn't reply. I wasn't about to discuss what happened the night before or this morning with Ava.

"Fine," she relented. "I won't ask you anything else."

Though neither of the women mentioned it, I decided to stay for the rest of the day. I wanted to protect not only Savannah, but Ava as well. For the first time in centuries, I wished for my sword.

When they fell out of fashion, I hadn't thought I would want it back, but I ached for its familiar weight against my side. I felt naked without it even though it had been at least three hundred years since I carried it.

I watched as Savannah made coffees and teas for customers. As the hours passed, I could see the toll her interactions with other people took on her. Her sparkling eyes became dull and her face grew pale.

It brought her words this morning back to the forefront of my mind. She insisted that I would be helping her if I took her excess emotions and, as I watched her, I was beginning to believe it. She was greatly affected by the people she saw each day and it wore her down.

After a few hours, the shop was empty and Savannah came over and sat next to me at the table.

"Hey," she greeted me, her voice subdued.

"Are you well?" I asked.

She rubbed her forehead with her fingertips. "Not really. I'm not used to working this many hours without a break. My head is beginning to ache and I have several readings to do this afternoon."

I could see the halo of red, brown, and black circling her head in her aura and I knew it was more than just a small pain.

"Come with me," I said, getting to my feet and holding out my hand.

She laid her palm against mine and allowed me to pull her to her feet. I nodded to Ava as I led Savannah into the niche where she performed tarot readings and pulled the curtain shut.

"What are you doing?" Savannah asked as I guided her into a chair.

"I want to try something." My gut twisted at the thought of what I was about to do, but I could clearly see Savannah's distress. I couldn't sit by and allow her to suffer.

"What?" she asked, her eyes wide. "Are you sure you're okay? Your face is pale."

I took a slow, controlled breath, trying to focus. "Yes, I'm fine, but I can see that you're not and I don't like that you're in pain." She opened her mouth to speak, but I shook my head. "No, I want to try to help you the way you suggested this morning. I want to ease your pain if I can."

She stared at me in surprise for a long moment before she asked, "Are you sure?"

I nodded and sat down next to her. "Now that I can see how people affect you, I want to do what I can to counteract that." I reached out to take her hands. "I need you to close your eyes and trust me," I said.

"I do trust you," she replied, her eyelids drifting shut.

"That's good because I trust you too," I replied. "First, I need you to open your mind to me. It's not necessary but it makes the process easier for both of us."

"Okay," she whispered.

Immediately, I could feel the barriers around her mind open and I could feel the churning emotions inside her, many of which weren't her own. I closed my eyes and focused on Savannah. With great care, I looked through the pain, anger, sadness, humor, and joy that I saw within her and I realized that not all of the feelings she picked up were negative.

"Do you still find it difficult to be around happy people?" I asked her, curious if I needed to remove those emotions as well.

"They aren't difficult to be around, but it does affect me. It makes me feel like I slammed a couple of shots of espresso and sometimes I can't sleep because of it," she answered.

It was surprising how easy it was to remove the excess of emotions inside her with her mind opened to me. Much easier than it usually was. As precisely as possible, I slowly siphoned off the riot of pain, happiness, and grief that swirled around her heart. I could feel my own strength increasing with each moment. When I reached the feelings that belonged to Savannah alone, I gradually withdrew, watching for any sign of discomfort from her. She didn't react at all, her breathing still even and her heartbeat steady.

When I was done, I opened my eyes and saw that the reddish brown color around her head was gone, leaving behind only the multicolored prism that usually surrounded her.

She took a deep breath and opened her eyes. I could see that the lively spark had returned to their dark brown depths.

"How do you feel?" I asked, still clasping her hands loosely in mine.

Savannah thought for a moment before she answered. "I feel good. Normal. And my headache is gone," she replied with a smile. Leaning forward, she kissed me. "Thank you, Rhys. I wasn't sure if I would be able to make it through today, but now I feel fine."

As I studied her face, I could see that she was telling the truth. She glowed once again.

The curtain swished softly as Ava stuck her head behind it. "I'm sorry to interrupt, but your first client is here, Savannah." Her eyes moved over Savannah's face. "You look better."

"I am better," Savannah replied as she got to her feet. She leaned over and kissed me one more time. "Thank you, Rhys."

She left the niche and I could hear her greeting her client. I rose from the chair, but Ava stepped in front of me before I could leave the room.

"I'm glad you helped her, Rhys," she whispered. "I was ready to fight her and send her home if necessary. I can't stand to see her hurting like that."

"I couldn't stand it either."

"You'll probably have to do it again in a couple of hours, you realize that right?" she asked.

I nodded. "I'll do whatever is necessary."

Ava smiled and stepped back. "I'm really glad I offered you my rental home, Rhys Carey. I knew you would be good for Savannah in some way, even if I wasn't expecting this." As we moved aside to allow Savannah and her client into the reading room, Ava crossed her arms over her chest. "I hate to say it," she muttered, "But I think I'm going to have to cut back hours for a while. School is out for the year and summers are slower, so I may go to half days during the week and a full day on Saturday."

"Will you be able to manage?" I asked, worried about her financial stability. I wanted to offer her help but I doubted she would accept it. When Cornelius died, I'd gained access to all his bank accounts. I had no idea how he'd accumulated such vast sums of money, but there was no way I could spend the contents of his bank accounts on just myself. I rarely bought anything other than food and the money just kept accruing interest. In the year since his death, the accounts had grown at an alarming rate, but I wasn't sure what to do with it all.

"Oh, I'll be fine. I just didn't want to close the shop because I was worried that Savannah might not be able to pay her bills without her income. She doesn't have to work full-time because of the trust her grandmother left her, but it's still a modest amount of money and I don't want her to get in a bind. She won't let me lend her money, so my only option was to keep the store open." She turned toward me. "Want a glass of iced tea?" she asked.

"Yes, please."

"Then come over here and let me show you how to make it."

I didn't argue. Sitting at a table for the past few hours hadn't been fun. I needed some activity to keep me busy.

As she walked me through the process of making iced tea with agave nectar and lemon, Savannah emerged from the reading room with her client. The woman she was with looked familiar but I couldn't place her. She walked the woman to the door and said good-bye, but didn't escort her to her vehicle as she usually would.

Though we hadn't discussed it, I was glad to see that she gave a thought to her safety.

"That was quick," Ava commented.

Savannah shrugged. "She got a call and had to leave suddenly."

"How's she doing?"

"Not well," Savannah said, her eyes sad. "She misses her husband."

I understood then how I recognized the woman. She was the client who had lost her husband recently.

Ava's cell phone rang and she grimaced at the screen. "It's one of the suppliers. I'm going to take this in my office because I don't think our customers need to hear me cuss out someone on the phone."

She put the phone to her ear and disappeared through the door that led to the storeroom.

"Do you want some tea?" I asked Savannah.

She shook her head and came over to me. I stood perfectly still as she wrapped her arms around my waist, curling her body into mine. Hesitantly, I put my arms around her, unable to get a clear read of what she was feeling.

"Is something wrong?" I asked her.

"No," she murmured, her cheek pressed against my chest.

"Did your client say something that upset you?"

Savannah pulled back a little and looked up at me. "Yes and no. She said something that made me think about life and how anything can happen. She told me that when she thinks of the day her husband died, what tortures her the most is that she didn't tell him she loved him before he left the house. She was distracted and busy and she didn't take the time to say it." Her voice caught as she continued. "It's heartbreaking to hear that."

I cupped her cheek. "I'm sorry, Savannah."

She stared up at me, her eyes shimmering with a thin sheen of tears. "I don't want that kind of regret. The regret of things left unsaid or undone. When she said that to me, I realized that I've been living half a life, letting fear keep me from doing and saying the things I truly wanted." Savannah took a deep breath, her gaze intent upon mine. "Last night, I realized that I love you, but I didn't say it because I was afraid it was too soon or you wouldn't reciprocate my feelings. But I also realized that none of that matters. Whether you feel the same way or not, it doesn't diminish what I feel for you. I don't want to wake up one day and wish that I'd said it because I no longer have the chance."

I lifted my other hand so that I held her face between my palms. "I told you that my heart beats for you, Savannah. Until I met you and loved you, I didn't think I had a heart or a soul. Now they're both yours. I love you and I never want you to believe that to be otherwise."

When I kissed her, I poured all the love I felt for her into the meeting of our lips. I wanted her to see into my heart.

Because it now belonged solely to her.

CHAPTER TWENTY-TWO

Savannah

MY LIFE HAD become pure bliss. Rhys and I were in love and living together. Every day, I learned something new about him. And every night, we explored each other's bodies before falling asleep with our limbs tangled together.

I felt as though all my dreams had come true.

Rhys came to work with me every day. He seemed to enjoy it. I could tell that the restriction of staying close to the store or home was beginning to wear on Ava. There was also something else bothering her. Every day she seemed paler and more withdrawn. I'd tried talking to her, but she kept brushing me off, which wasn't like her.

Today, she seemed even more distracted, constantly checking her phone and unable to stand still. When she disappeared into the storeroom, I walked over to the table where Rhys sat reading a book and plopped down in his lap.

"I need you to do something for me," I told him.

He smiled up at me. "Anything."

I narrowed my eyes. "Anything? That's a dangerous offer."

Rhys' smile widened and his blue eyes sparkled with mischief. "Okay, almost anything."

"Will you go into the storeroom with Ava and see if you can

get her to talk about what's bugging her? She's not herself and she won't tell me."

"What makes you think she'll talk to me about it if she won't talk to you?" he asked.

"Because I'm worried that she thinks she's protecting me. She considers you her partner when it comes to keeping me safe. Though I don't understand why she feels that way. I may not have the power or skills that she has, but I'm not completely defense-less." I shook my head. "But that doesn't matter. I just want to make sure she's okay and if she won't talk to me, maybe she'll share it with you."

Rhys looked undecided.

"Just go in and check on her. I'm worried." I truly hoped Ava would at least unload a little of whatever was bothering her. It had to be serious if she wouldn't even discuss it with me.

"Fine," Rhys sighed, lifting me off his lap. "I'll go talk to her, but if she tells me it's none of my concern, I'm taking her at her word. Which you should do too," he admonished.

"Normally, I would, but she's not acting like herself."

He kissed my lips and murmured, "I'll be right back. Stay inside the store."

I barely refrained from rolling my eyes because I already knew to stay inside. I didn't need to be told. There was an itch between my shoulder blades when I was at the store, a sensation of being watched. I knew something was coming, but I wasn't sure when.

Rhys disappeared into the storeroom and I grabbed a cloth and disinfectant from behind the counter. The shop was slow today and I decided to clean since the tables were empty. I started with the booth closest to the door, spraying the table down and wiping it with the damp towel.

Suddenly, the windows seemed to melt away and the wall be-neath disappeared. Before I could move, two long arms reached through the space and took hold of me. I gripped the bottle of disinfectant tightly, pointing it the direction of my attacker's face and sprayed it several times.

The man swore, his hands releasing me, and I took three stumbling steps back. I turned to flee, drawing in a breath to scream, when a hand clamped down over my mouth and an arm circled my waist.

I was yanked off my feet and back into a rock solid body.

"Stupid move, Savannah," a low male voice whispered in my ear. "Now you've pissed me off."

I tried to scream as Macgrath carried me backward through the portal. Though my struggle was fruitless against the vampire's strength, I fought his hold with all my might as I watched the wall in front of us close up brick by brick and the window shift into place.

Then I felt a sickening lurch in my stomach and the sensation of falling through the air, only my feet remained planted on solid ground.

When the whirling colors around me stopped, I heaved, struggling to hold back the sickness that wanted to rise from my belly. My head spun wildly and my legs gave out beneath me.

With nearly gentle hands, Macgrath deposited me onto a sofa, tucking a pillow behind me. "Take slow, deep breaths," he commanded. "And don't close your eyes because it will only make it worse."

I swallowed back another gag and focused on my breathing, hoping that I wouldn't embarrass myself and puke everywhere. I didn't even notice that Macgrath disappeared until he returned with a glass of ginger ale.

"Drink this. The sugar and the bubbles will help."

I stared at the glass with suspicion, not wanting to take it.

With a heavy sigh, he lifted it to his lips and took a healthy swallow. "It's not poisoned or drugged or anything."

"Even if it was," I replied, lifting my defiant gaze to his. "You wouldn't die if you drank it."

"Do you want to feel better or not?" he asked, holding out the glass to me again.

I shook my head. "I'll only drink it if you bring me an unopened bottle or can."

Macgrath stared down at me for a moment then he burst into laughter. "Oh, you're a feisty one, aren't you?"

"I'm not feisty. I'm pissed," I retorted. "But I'm not going to bother talking to you about it because I know that you're just the minion that does Rhiannon's dirty work. So until she's here, I'd prefer not to speak to you."

His smile faded, replaced with an unreadable expression. Without a word, he carried the glass out of the room. I looked around, searching for a clue about my whereabouts or an escape route. Even if I found one, I was still too light-headed to run. I wouldn't get more than three steps out of the room before I would puke or faint, or both.

To my surprise, Macgrath returned with a chilled can of soda and held it out to me. "This hasn't been tampered with. You'll feel much better after you have some sugar and caffeine."

Warily, I took the can from him. Though it was a small act of rebellion, I didn't thank him. The vampire didn't deserve my courtesy considering he'd kidnapped me right out of *The Magic Bean*.

I cracked open the can and sipped the soda, letting the sweet flavor and the bite of the bubbles settle my stomach and my head. Within moments I did feel better.

Unable to contain myself, I took in my surroundings and asked, "Where's your boss?"

Macgrath raised a single brow and I frowned at him, wondering how he did that. When I attempted that eye trick, I looked like I had a strange tic.

"She'll be here later," he replied. "She had some business to attend to."

My muscles tightened. "Business? With Ava and Rhys?"

The vampire just smiled smugly. "That's not something you need to know."

I stared at him, wondering if I had the guts to show him exactly what I was capable of. Unfortunately, I'd forgotten that most vampires were able to read minds if a person wasn't careful enough to shield their thoughts.

"What *are* you capable of?" he asked, his tone sardonic.

I leaned back against the pillow he'd placed behind me and crossed my arms over my chest. "You'll find out eventually," I replied.

Macgrath leaned one hip against the bar that separated the living area from a sleek, modern kitchen. "If I think for a single moment that you're trying to hurt me, I will kill you," he growled. "Do you think you're fast enough to stop a vampire before he breaks your neck?"

I knew that I wasn't but I wouldn't tell him that. Instead, I tilted my chin up and stared straight at him, refusing to back down.

Once again the vampire shocked me with his reaction. He laughed. "I don't think Rhiannon understood what she was getting into when she decided to use you as her leverage," he murmured. "If she did, there's no way she would have followed through."

I wondered what his cryptic words meant but I wouldn't give him the satisfaction of asking. I let my eyes wander over my surroundings and realized I was in some sort of house. It was what I would call a modern monstrosity. The floors and walls were concrete and the furnishings were so sleek and unadorned that they were boring. The entire living room and kitchen completely lacked any sort of personality, unless 'cold' was a type of interior design. But at least the couch was comfortable.

"Where are we?" I asked even though I doubted he would tell me.

"Rhiannon's house."

His immediate answer surprised me, especially since it was the truth.

When he saw my face, he chuckled. "It's not that easy to find," he continued.

I studied the interior with new eyes. If this was Rhiannon's home, it said a great deal about her state of mind. She had no delusions of grandeur. She didn't want flash or recognition. The house might be large and the furnishings well made, but she didn't invest a lot of money into her home, even though she had it.

She didn't live here so much as exist within the walls. I loathed admitting it, but Rhiannon Temple and I had a lot in common. While I lived half a life, she didn't live at all.

"Don't feel sorry for her, Savannah," Macgrath stated, his voice a low growl. "She doesn't deserve it. Any pain she carries, she brought upon herself."

I thought of Rhys and Cornelius. Neither of them asked for their pain. While Rhys managed to remain generous and good, Cornelius let the darkness swallow him. I wondered if Rhiannon's experiences had done the same for her.

"Savannah." I looked up when the vampire called my name. "For some people, the darkness already lives inside them, looking for an excuse to get out. When they find it, they relish the chaos they create."

I didn't argue, but I did wonder if Rhiannon had welcomed the darkness within her or if she'd had no other choice but to accept it.

CHAPTER TWENTY-THREE

Rhys

THE STOREROOM WAS empty when I entered, though light escaped from beneath the door of Ava's office. I knocked once and waited for her to grant me permission to come in, but she was silent.

I turned the knob and pushed it opened. Ava sat at her desk, her head bowed as she stared down at her phone. Her finger tapped the side in a slow, steady rhythm as though she were marking time.

"Ava?"

Her head came up when I said her name. "Hey, Rhys. What's up?"

"I think that's my question for you," I replied.

Her gaze skittered away from mine. "I'm fine."

"I think we both know that's bullshit," I stated as I shut the door behind me and moved to the single chair that faced her desk.

The legs creaked ominously as I settled my weight into the seat. Leaning back, I laced my fingers over my abdomen and waited.

"Margaret was supposed to call me yesterday morning and she didn't. I can't get in touch with her." Her finger kept tapping the side of the phone. "I've been trying to call her for two days. I have a bad feeling about this."

"Do you think something happened to her?"

"I'm almost certain it did," Ava murmured. She looked up at me again. "I've tried scrying for her location with a mirror, but I've never met her in person and that makes it more difficult. Do you think Kerry can find someone to check on her?"

"I'll call her now," I offered.

Before I could reach into my pocket for my phone, a shrill sound pierced the air. Ava and I leapt to our feet. "Someone's broken through the wards," she cried, ripping the door to the office open and sprinting through the storeroom.

I followed close on her heels as she burst through the doors that lead back into the shop. She stopped short and I nearly crashed into her back.

The cafe was orderly and neat, the tables lined up properly and the shelves were untouched. The bar gleamed as usual. The scent of scorched paper filled the air but nothing was aflame. The only thing out of place was a single chair lying on the floor on its side.

And Savannah was nowhere to be found.

Quickly, I moved around Ava and checked the reading room, the bathroom, and anywhere else that Savannah might have hidden. She was gone.

I turned toward Ava. "We have to find Savannah," I insisted.

She nodded. "We will, but first we need to know who took her."

I watched as she lifted her hands in a wide, sweeping motion. Before us a pale grey version of Savannah stood in front of one of the tables, spraying it with disinfectant before wiping it down. Then the wall in front of her split apart, revealing a man. He stepped through the opening and I saw his face clearly. It was Macgrath.

A rage I'd never experienced before filled me. It burned hot and bright, swelling to the point that I didn't think I could contain it. I smelled the electricity and knew that power sparked from my fingertips. Curling my hands into fists, I focused on the scene that unfolded in front of me.

Macgrath grabbed Savannah. She twisted and fought before bringing the bottle up and spraying the vampire in the face. When he released her, she turned and took two steps away before he was on her again. I could see the absolute fear on her face and the wrath inside me doubled.

The vampire wrapped one arm around her waist and clapped a hand over her mouth as he dragged her backward out of the portal. The wall closed in on itself, leaving nothing behind but the overturned chair.

Ava waved her arms again and the smoky grey shadows disappeared. "Well, we know who has her," she muttered. "Now, we just have to find them and kill them."

I couldn't agree more.

FINDING MACGRATH AND Rhiannon proved to be more difficult than I believed it would be.

Ava stood over the table, a crystal on a chain dangled from her fingertips. A map was spread out beneath her hands, but the crystal merely swayed, never stopping over a specific point.

"Fuck," Ava cursed, dropping the chain on the tabletop. "This is the fourth map we've tried and I can't find them anywhere."

"She must be using a spell to mask their location," I stated.

Ava's eyes were pure, brilliant purple when she looked up at me. Her stare clearly stated that she'd already considered that.

"The bitch is good," she mumbled. "I've broken more masking spells than most witches ever cast but I can't break hers."

"There must be something else we can do," I insisted.

"There is," Ava replied. "But it will take time. Time we don't have."

"Then what the fuck are we supposed to do?" I growled.

She rubbed her forehead. "If I had something that belonged to her, it would be a lot easier. Or if I had a way to boost my power, I might be able to manage it."

Her words gave me an idea. Kerry and Finn often fed each other power when they needed it. I didn't bother asking Ava if she was willing. For Savannah, I knew she would be.

Pulling my phone out of my pocket, I dialed Kerry.

"I need your help," I said as soon as she picked up the phone.

"I know. And the answer is yes." She hesitated. "When this is all over, we need to talk."

Triumph surged through me. "I'm going to give the phone to Ava. Just tell her what you need her to do. Anything else we need to talk about can wait."

Without waiting for her response, I held my cell out to Ava.

As I expected, she took it and lifted it to her ear. "Hi, Kerry. I'm Ava Amaris. Rhys said you could help us."

The urge to destroy roiled inside of me. The woman I intended to make my wife was at the mercy of a vampire and a dark witch. We had to find her before it was too late.

CHAPTER TWENTY-FOUR

Savannah

STARING DOWN AT the ground, I rethought my plan to climb out of the bathroom window. I hadn't realized that we were on the second floor when I told Macgrath I needed to pee. Now, the ground seemed very far away.

Then I thought of Rhys and Ava. They would be worried about me and, if they came looking for me, I feared they would both do something they regretted. Macgrath and Rhiannon might deserve to be punished for what they did, but I didn't want the weight of their pain on Rhys' soul.

I took a deep breath, pulled up my skirt, and threw my leg over the windowsill. I wished I'd worn something other than my usual summer dress. Moving carefully, I turned so that my belly was against the sill and reached back with my foot. There was a concrete ledge running the length of the house so I placed my toes on it. Gingerly, I put my weight down on my foot and brought my other leg out. Once I had both feet on the ledge, I looked down. If I let myself hang from my extended arms, I would only be four or five feet from the ground. At least that's what I told myself. I also decided that once this was over, I was going to start working out. My arms and legs trembled from the effort of holding myself on this ledge.

The wind blew, lifting my skirt and obscuring my view of the grass below. Taking a deep breath, I prepared to put my plan into action.

"Nice panties," a male voice murmured. "Does the bra match?"

I shrieked and my hands slipped off the window. My legs wouldn't hold my weight and I fell backwards away from the wall. I closed my eyes, knowing that it was going to hurt badly when I hit the ground.

The air whooshed out of my lungs when I hit, but it wasn't grass beneath me. Two strong arms caught me, one at my mid-back and the other beneath my knees. I stared up at Macgrath's annoyed face for a beat before I went into action.

I thrashed in his arms, screaming my head off in hopes that someone would hear me. I scratched him and hit him with my fists as I kicked my legs. The vampire grunted as he released my legs, wrapping both arms around me in an effort to contain my struggles.

"You motherfucking asshole," I yelled, kicking his shins with my now freed feet. "You're a goddamn dick-faced bastard! Let me go!" More curses streamed from my lips as I fought like a mad thing. I said things that would have made my grandmother faint. But if there was ever a time to cut loose, it was now.

"Do you kiss your mother with that mouth?" he asked, jerking his head back to avoid my flying fist. Suddenly, he had enough and gave me a firm shake. "Stop fighting. We're a half hour away from the nearest house by car. Even if I did let you go, you wouldn't get far."

The fight went out of me then and I let my body go limp.

"That's better," he stated with a nod, letting my feet touch the ground. "Now, let's go inside."

Thirty minutes later, I was seated on the couch, my elbow resting on the arm and my cheek propped on my hand. Apparently Rhiannon didn't believe in television and there wasn't a single bookshelf in sight. To my utter disbelief, I was bored nearly senseless now that I knew the vampire guarding me had no intention of hurting me. At least not yet.

He'd proven that when he caught me climbing out of the bathroom window. Even as I fought, he'd been almost gentle when he restrained me. I bit, clawed, and cursed at him with the expansive vocabulary of a sailor. I used words that I'd never said before because my grandmother would have washed my mouth out with soap if she even thought I uttered them. He hadn't even left a bruise on my skin and seemed utterly unperturbed.

Macgrath flipped the page of his book, ignoring me completely. I had no idea where he got the book from but the language on the cover wasn't English, so I was pretty sure I wouldn't be able to read it even if he was polite enough to offer it to me. I wasn't sure but it looked like French.

I sighed and shifted my butt on the sofa cushions.

"What's wrong now?" he asked absently, his eyes moving steadily over the page.

"Other than you kidnapping me, you mean?" I asked him belligerently, crossing my arms over my chest. Strangely, since the bathroom window incident, I was no longer afraid of him. He'd had every opportunity to harm me then and he hadn't.

"Yes, other than that." His voice was mild as though we were talking about the weather rather than the fact that he had forcibly taken me from *The Magic Bean*.

"I'm bored and I'm hungry. So if there's no TV or books around here, then the least you can do is feed me."

His eyes lifted then, focusing on me. "You're probably hungry because you expended all that energy calling me names earlier."

I shook my head. "No, it's my dinner time. You're obligated to feed me."

The corners of his mouth twitched and I knew he was trying not to smile. "Obligated?"

I shrugged. "I wouldn't be here if you hadn't grabbed me from the coffee shop. Therefore you're required to feed me."

"I'm not required to do anything," he replied, going back to his book.

"Fine," I said, crossing my legs. "Maybe I'll sing. Do you like *Ninety-Nine Bottles of Beer on the Wall?*"

His book closed with a snap. "I'll see what I can find."

I smiled smugly behind his back.

"Get your ass in here and help me. I don't trust you not to try and run off again."

I got to my feet and followed him into the kitchen. I sat at the bar as he studied the contents of the fridge. In turn, I studied him. He was good-looking, clearly intelligent, and strong. I sensed no evil from him. I couldn't understand why he was working with Rhiannon.

"Go ahead and ask," he said as he turned from the fridge with a package of mushrooms in his hand.

"How did you know I wanted to ask you a question?" I queried.

He tapped his temple with his free hand. "You're thinking so loudly that I can practically hear you even though you're not speaking. Just ask me whatever it is so I can get some peace and quiet."

I rolled my eyes. He acted tough and abrasive, but his behavior with me and his emotions, what few I could discern, told a different story. "Why are you helping Rhiannon? You're not evil, I could feel it if you were. And you don't enjoy causing pain. So what do you get from this?"

He tossed the mushrooms next to the sink and braced his

hands on the counter. "You don't beat around the bush, do you?"

I shook my head. "But you're evading my question."

He ripped open the package of mushrooms and began taking them out one by one. "She has something I need."

I studied his face then looked deeper. Whatever it was, it was vital to him. I could sense his regret and his desire to be free of her hold.

"What's that?" I asked.

"The name of my maker."

"You don't know who made you?" That was strange. Most vampires had close relationships with their creators. It was considered an important relationship in vampire culture, similar to that of a parent and child. Or in the case of mates, a husband and wife.

He shook his head, and to my utter shock, answered my question. "I-I can't remember," he replied. "I can't remember anything about when I was turned or even before. I woke up one day and knew nothing, not even my own name. I was fully grown, but couldn't recall my childhood. Then the first time I needed to feed..." He trailed off, his jaw clenching. "I need to find my maker and find out why they abandoned me with no memories in a land that I didn't understand."

Sympathy welled inside me. I couldn't imagine waking up one day without a name or friends and family. The very idea scared the heck out of me.

"Don't pity me," he said gruffly. "I've done well enough."

I pushed my sympathy for him aside. This man had kidnapped me. He didn't deserve pity, even with a story like that. "How long have you been with Rhiannon?"

"A few years," he answered cryptically, his attention on the mushrooms as he cleaned them.

I stared at him in consternation. Macgrath wasn't stupid. How could he believe after years with Rhiannon that she still intended to help him?

He stopped what he was doing and turned his eyes to me. "You're doing it again."

"Doing what?" I asked in confusion.

"Thinking so loudly that I can nearly hear every word." He sighed and reached beneath the counter for a cutting board and knife. He began to chop the mushrooms.

I watched as he sliced the mushrooms neatly then turned and took an onion from a basket on the counter. He removed the skin and chopped it as well.

Finally, he said, "I know she isn't going to help me."

"Then why are you still here?"

"Because I have nowhere else to go."

I couldn't imagine that feeling. Despite the problems my abilities caused me, I had friends and family to help me if I needed it. Though I often felt alone, I wasn't. Not truly. Not in the way that Macgrath had been and still was.

I didn't say anything else as Macgrath took the ingredients to the gas range and began putting together a meal.

A few minutes later, the front door opened and Rhiannon sauntered inside, looking cool and fresh despite the heat outside.

"Good evening," she greeted me pleasantly, as though I were an invited guest rather than a victim of a kidnapping.

She didn't wait for my reply, moving directly toward Macgrath. "Darling, you're making dinner. It smells fantastic."

Rhiannon stopped next to him and rose on her toes to kiss his cheek. Even from across the kitchen, I could see his body tense beneath her touch and feel his repulsion.

"Rhiannon," he greeted her as he sidestepped her hand.

A swell of emotions filled the room, but they weren't Macgrath's. Anger, pain, and desperation took over the space. I stared at Rhiannon in shock at the amount of chaos that surrounded her. I immediately understood that she wasn't hiding her abilities right now. Her pale skin glowed with an inner light and her dark eyes shimmered with power. I was also surprised at the loneliness that filled every part of her soul. Rhiannon might have been a powerful witch, but she was also an innately damaged woman. Sympathy filled me for her emotions weren't so different from mine.

The tempest inside her suddenly quieted as though she slammed a door between us.

Then she smiled and I began to rethink my assessment of her because the smile was malicious and calculating.

"I think it's time we made a phone call, don't you?"

She reached into her bag and removed her cell phone. After pressing a few buttons, she put it to her ear.

"Hello, Ava. I believe we have a few things to discuss." I could hear the sound of Ava's voice from across the room and Rhiannon's smile widened. "Now, now, is that any way to talk to someone who's hosting your friend?" She paused briefly. "I didn't think so. I believe you know that I want the *animavore*. I'm going to give you some coordinates in a few moments and you will bring him to me at ten tonight. If you're late or you pull any kind of shit, Macgrath will rip the little empath's throat out. Is that understood?"

Without waiting for a response, Rhiannon disconnected the call and leveled her eyes on me. "The same goes for you, Savannah. If you try any sort of stunt, I'll peel the skin from the witch's bones and make you watch."

Rhiannon Temple might be a writhing pit of despair and emptiness, but she was still evil. She wasn't deserving of my compassion.

CHAPTER TWENTY-FIVE

Savannah

M Y HEART BEAT a fast tattoo against my ribs as Macgrath steered Rhiannon's Land Rover down a gravel road. We'd been driving for a while, heading toward the middle of nowhere it seemed.

After Rhiannon called Ava, she disappeared into another part of the house and came back wearing a pair of jeans, boots, and a black shirt with the sleeves rolled up. That should have been my first clue of what was to come.

Then she insisted we sit down and eat dinner together, as though she were hosting a dinner party. She set the table with white square plates and water goblets. There were even candles and a small centerpiece of burgundy calla lilies.

Macgrath dished out servings of mushroom risotto and roasted asparagus while Rhiannon poured out glasses of chardonnay. We sat around that table and ate the food in silence. Though I hadn't been lying when I told Macgrath I was hungry, I couldn't eat. I pushed the risotto around on the plate, thinking about Rhys. I knew that I would be freaking out right about now if I were in his shoes. I was sure he was doing the same.

When the meal was over, Macgrath washed the dishes and Rhiannon disappeared again.

At a quarter to nine, she came back into the living room. "It's time to go."

We'd been on the road for nearly forty-five minutes when Macgrath turned off the gravel road and drove down a narrow dirt trail. It definitely wasn't a road. More like a track that had been worn through the woods.

Finally, he stopped the Land Rover and put it in park. He looked over his shoulder at me. "We're here."

I climbed out of the vehicle and felt a shiver run over my skin. Though we were in the middle of nowhere, there was no sound. Not a single insect or bird made a noise. There wasn't even a breeze to stir the leaves.

Something was very wrong here.

Macgrath took my arm at the elbow and set off through the trees until we reached a clearing. The moon didn't pierce the canopy created by the trees and he didn't use a flashlight, yet he walked through the woods as though he could see perfectly.

However, I couldn't. I tripped over rocks and branches, nearly twisting my ankle when I stepped in a low spot. With a heavy sigh, Macgrath stopped and swung me up in his arms. I squirmed and shoved at his shoulders.

"Put me down," I insisted.

His arms squeezed me tightly enough to push the air out of my lungs. "Quiet. If you break an ankle, I'll have to carry you anyway and you'll be in a lot more pain."

I smacked his shoulder. "Can't. Breathe," I gasped.

His arms loosened but he didn't put me down. I huffed and crossed my arms over my chest. Over his shoulder, I caught a glimpse of Rhiannon's face. She wasn't happy with the situation. At all.

"Can we get on with it?" she asked, putting her hands on her hips.

Once again Macgrath's hands tightened on me, but only just a little. Though his emotions were tightly leashed, I could feel a flare of anger toward Rhiannon. He resumed walking, carrying me as though I weighed nothing.

Since I didn't have to worry about watching where I was walking, I stared ahead into the darkness and thought about Rhys and what was happening. I couldn't let him give himself up to Rhiannon for me. I would never be able to live with myself.

I didn't have Macgrath's strength or the power that Ava and Rhys had. There was only one thing I could do to stop this and everything within me repelled the idea. Despite what everyone believed, I wasn't completely helpless.

Ava had been right when she said that emotions were part of the soul. And the soul was necessary for survival. If I drew on Rhiannon's emotions, draining them from her, I would also be taking her soul. I probably wouldn't be able to kill her, but I could weaken her enough so that Rhys or Ava could. I had to give them a chance to help me because there was no way in hell I was letting the man I loved give himself up for me. I also couldn't believe that I was thinking so calmly about the possibility of snuffing out someone's life. I had always tried to use my abilities to help people rather than hurt them.

Then I thought of Rhys and all the pain he'd been through, all the pain that Rhiannon likely had planned, and my resolve hardened. I would do whatever necessary to protect Rhys, even kill.

Macgrath emerged from the trees into a large field and he put me on my feet without a word. His jaw was clenched and I feared that I'd been thinking too loudly and he'd heard it all.

"Don't move," he commanded.

I stood still and watched as Rhiannon walked around, murmuring beneath her breath while light spilled from her palms. A large glowing circle formed on the ground, about twenty feet in diameter, leaving the three of us in the center.

I felt the weight of the magic surrounding me, and my heart sank. Ava was strong but I didn't think she was powerful enough to break this spell.

"Why are you doing this?" I asked Rhiannon. "Why do you want Rhys?"

At first I thought she was going to ignore me because she continued what she was doing without answering. Then she murmured, "He has something I want."

"What could he have that you want?"

Her eyes came to me, the dark depths piercing and cold. "Power. Power like I've never seen."

I shook my head. I'd never seen Rhys exhibit magic on that level. "You have to be mistaken."

Rhiannon laughed and it raised goose bumps on my skin. "You have no idea what you've had in your bed, do you?" she queried. "The *animavore* is the key to what I want. I helped create him for that singular purpose and Gaius betrayed me."

"You helped *make* him?"

"He was my finest creation. I intended to create another such as Macgrath, but my magic wouldn't comply, but Cornelius and Rhys proved to be a far better substitute. They would have helped me achieve my goal."

"And what's that?" My voice was soft, barely above a whisper.

"I will be a goddess, a being so powerful that all will tremble before me."

I stared at her and shook my head. "And what use is that? What use is all that power if you hoard it for yourself rather than helping others?"

"Helping others?" she scoffed. "I spent decades helping others, giving them everything I had to offer, sharing the gifts I'd been given. Do you know what they did to me?" she asked, stalking closer. "When I fell ill, after all that time spent helping them, they left me alone to die. No one came to aid me when I was in need. I was old and weak but none of the people I helped, the people I *loved*, could be bothered to feed me or keep my fires burning as I had done for them hundreds, nay thousands of times."

"How are you here?" I asked.

Her eyes burned with frigid fire. "On my deathbed, I cast a spell. I recalled every drop of power I expended to help the villagers. Everyone I healed, everyone I ever helped, no longer benefitted from my aid."

"What happened to them?"

"Most died. Some were able to survive, but they learned that they shouldn't have taken me for granted."

I shook my head. I could understand her bitterness at being abandoned by the villagers she'd helped so much, but to kill them in retaliation? "Do you truly believe the punishment fit the crime?"

Rhiannon waved a hand. "It doesn't matter if it did or not. I no longer concern myself with the *help* people might need. What I want is what matters."

"What do you expect all this power to bring you?" I truly wanted to understand. "Do you want people to bow down to you? To serve you?"

"Bow down to me, yes, that sounds nice," Rhiannon laughed. "But I have no desire to be empress of this realm."

I frowned at her strange word choice. "Then why do you want all this power?"

The manic light in her eyes faded slightly, replaced once again by the pain I sensed roiling inside her. "There is one who made me what I am, for every creature has a maker. She abandoned me in my time of need and then punished me for doing what was necessary to save myself. She doesn't deserve to sit in judgment of me or of anyone. My magic is not for her to give and take."

I stared at her in disbelief. "All of this is for revenge?" I questioned. "You want to punish your maker so you're killing people? Do you not see how crazy that is?"

The witch scowled at me, the power swirling around her as she lifted her hand. "You—"

"They're coming," Macgrath said, stepping between us.

Still glowering at me, Rhiannon moved toward the edge of the circle. I watched the headlights that halted on the road that ran along the edge of the field and felt my heart thud against my ribs.

I could feel the energy gathering around us as the headlights shut off. From across the pasture, I could hear the doors slam as they climbed out and began walking toward us. The ground trembled beneath us as a light encircled the entire field, radiating upward until it closed high above us, creating a pulsing dome of glowing magic.

I'd known since the moment I stepped out of Rhiannon's car that something wasn't right. Now I knew why.

The trap was ready and waiting and now Rhiannon Temple had sprung it around us.

There would be no escape unless we defeated her.

CHAPTER TWENTY-SIX

Rhys

A S THE DOME of light formed over us, I looked over at Ava. "I should have traced to them."

Ava shook her head and lifted a hand, pointing to where I could see three figures waiting. Another circle, this one about twenty feet across pulsed with red light. "That's a very nasty protection spell," she stated softly. "If you managed to get tangled up in it, you would have been burned to a crisp or something worse."

I shrugged. "Maybe, or maybe not. She wants me alive, doesn't she?"

"It doesn't matter now," Ava replied. "We're here and we're trapped. We have to figure out a way to get past Rhiannon's spells before we can put a plan in motion."

In truth there was no plan. Kerry had been unable to help us locate Rhiannon or Savannah. She was insistent that we talk, that she had important information, but it would have to wait. If Rhiannon hadn't called Ava, we still wouldn't know where Savannah was or if she was unharmed. The only accord we had been able to come to was that Ava would deal with Rhiannon and I would kill Macgrath. As we approached the red circle, I could see that she was fine, standing unaided but clearly frightened.

Her body grew rigid when she saw me and I could practically feel her fear and relief even through the shield of magic that surrounded her. The rage that I'd suppressed all day grew, threatening to break free of my control. My fingertips burned as electricity danced between them. Savannah was terrified and I couldn't reach her.

Ava and I stopped a few feet away from the group. Rhiannon's face was lit with the scarlet glow, giving her a sinister appearance. It was the only time since the day she came to Savannah's house, she resembled the sorceress from my nightmares. The carefully crafted, sophisticated facade was gone. In its place was a witch full of bitterness and scorn. Macgrath stood behind her, his face partially shadowed and expression implacable.

For the first time in centuries, I wanted to cause pain and spill blood. I killed Cornelius to escape him, but I hadn't wanted to do it. Tonight, I craved it.

"I'm glad you two could make it," Rhiannon greeted us pleasantly.

I bit back the growl that built in my throat, letting Ava do the talking as we had discussed.

"We're here as you demanded," Ava replied. "Let Savannah leave."

Rhiannon smiled. It was cutting and cold, like the sharp steel blade of a battleax. "You and I both know that none of you will leave here tonight."

"Maybe," Ava said. "Or maybe you're wrong."

The evil bitch laughed, throwing her head back as though Ava's words were a joke that she found incredibly amusing. "I don't think so."

"This is your last chance," Ava warned. "If you stop now, I might not kill you."

Rhiannon shook her head, still chuckling. "There is no way you could defeat me."

Ava's only answer was to lift her arms. A wind lifted in the field, causing the knee-high grass to shift. The sound of the stalks rubbing together was like a hushed whisper, a thousand voices speaking quietly around us. Power prickled along my flesh, making my hair stand on end. The breeze intensified, the whispers growing louder, as it rushed from the outside edges of the field toward us.

I turned toward Ava, shocked to see the change in her appearance. Her golden hair and skin glowed, gleaming with an inner light. Her eyes were brilliant amethyst, sparking with magic. As the wind swirled around her, becoming a gale, her hair billowed behind her and her feet slowly lifted from the ground. She was more than a mere witch. She was one with the Goddess.

The smile faded from Rhiannon's face, her dark gaze narrowing. "The Goddess cannot help you here, Aveta of the Glade."

Behind Rhiannon, Macgrath's head jerked as she spoke, as though the strange name she used took him by surprise. Then, he stared up at Ava with narrowed eyes.

"I don't know who you're talking to, bitch, my name is Ava Amaris and I'm going to kick your ass." Lifting one arm, Ava turned her palm toward the red shield surrounding Rhiannon, Macgrath, and Savannah. White light streamed from her hand and slammed into the circle. There was a shower of sparks and the crackle of electricity as the spells clashed.

Rhiannon smiled once again as the red circle never wavered. "You can't break this spell, Ava. You aren't strong enough."

Ava tried again, another explosion of sparks shooting up into the night sky.

While Rhiannon was distracted, I inched closer to the circle, looking for a way to break through. I put my fingers against the pulsing light and hissed when they burned. I had never seen a spell like this before and even with my knowledge and power, I instinctively understood that I couldn't break it.

A movement behind Rhiannon caught my attention. I watched in horror as Savannah stepped closer to the witch, her gaze utterly focused. I recognized that look. I'd seen it often enough after she completed a tarot reading. She was siphoning Rhiannon's emotions.

The witch was too distracted with Ava to notice, but Macgrath stood next to Savannah, watching her dispassionately. He seemed to comprehend what she was doing, but he made no move to stop her. Suddenly, Rhiannon faltered, her hand lifting to her chest. The light circling her dimmed.

I glanced back at Savannah and clenched my fists when I saw how pale her face had become. She wasn't just drawing emotions from Rhiannon, but her very life. If she continued, she would end up doing irreparable damage to herself. I wanted to stop Savannah but there was no way I could reach her.

"Ava," I murmured, desperation rising within me.

"I know," she replied, lifting her hand again.

Rhiannon turned, looking over her shoulder, and her eyes locked on Savannah. "You think you can harm me?" she cried. "You think you can kill me?"

Macgrath stepped between the witch and the woman I loved. "Enough, Rhiannon. This has gone on for too long. I told you I would no longer obey your orders blindly after I learned what you've been doing. I will not stand by and watch you murder an innocent woman."

"You think you can stop me?" Rhiannon asked, moving closer to Macgrath, her posture threatening.

The red light around them dimmed again and I knew that Savannah was still drawing energy from Rhiannon. I also knew that she wouldn't last much longer. If Rhiannon didn't get to her, the stress of what she was doing would make her collapse. Macgrath blocked her from my sight but I knew that this was taking a toll on her.

"Now, Ava."

This time when the white light erupted from Ava's palm, the circle broke with a scream. Rhiannon cried out, falling to her knees.

"No!" she shrieked.

I advanced on her, planning to finish the job that Savannah had begun, but she lifted her hands, muttering beneath her breath. Throwing her arms out to the side, she vanished in a flash of red and a wisp of smoke.

"Dammit!" Ava yelled, dropping to the ground and running to the spot where Rhiannon vanished. "Son of a bitch!" She stood over the spot with her eyes closed, muttering to herself. Whatever she was attempting to do didn't work because she opened her eyes and glared at Macgrath. "I should kill you on the spot, but I need you to find her."

"I don't know where she is," he replied. He whirled in a blur of motion and caught Savannah as she sank to the ground.

My ire at him forgotten for the moment, I rushed to Savannah's side and crouched down. "Savannah," I murmured, taking her hand.

"Rhys," she whispered. "You're safe."

I could feel the wild tangle of emotions within her, the boiling anger and bitterness that she had taken from Rhiannon. As I had done before, I let those feelings flow into me, taking them from her. This time I could feel bits and pieces of Rhiannon's magic buried within them, as though her magic was fueled by the depth of her rage.

As I took it in, I felt my own strength grow. When I was done, I released Savannah's hand and helped her sit up, pulling her into my lap and holding her close.

"I'm okay," she murmured into my ear. "I'm fine."

"Don't ever do anything like that again," I commanded her as I held her tighter. "I've never been so fucking afraid in my life."

"Your woman has more courage than wisdom," Macgrath said from his crouch beside us.

I glanced up at him and blinked rapidly. A shimmering chain of magic seemed to emerge from the center of his chest. The chain was suspended in the air and disappeared into Ava's torso. Neither of them seemed aware of the magical bond, but it was there all the same.

"I should kill you," Ava sneered.

"No!" Savannah yelled from my lap. She scrambled to her feet as the vampire straightened from his crouch. "No killing. Macgrath saved me and he didn't hurt me."

"He kidnapped you!" Ava argued, her hands glowing as she gathered her magic.

"He also saved me," Savannah retorted.

"I have to agree with Ava," I declared as I rose from the ground. "He not only kidnapped you but he's helped Rhiannon kill other witches, shifters, and vampires."

Macgrath shook his head. "I've done a lot of things I'm not proud of, but I never helped Rhiannon kill innocent people. She swore to me that the rumors were just that and I believed her until recently. Since you came to Austin, Rhys, her behavior became more erratic. I realized then that she is an accomplished liar and I'd allowed my desperation to cloud my judgment."

Ava's eyes narrowed on him. "That answer is too pat. You're a vampire. You should have been able to sense her thoughts. Or at least some of them."

I nodded because it sounded too contrite to be true.

The vampire sighed and his shoulders slumped. "You just saw how powerful she is. Do you think she couldn't shield her thoughts from me? That she couldn't hide? She understood my weakness and took advantage of it. I'd been alone in this world for too long and she claimed to have the knowledge I sought. I would have believed anything she said if it meant she could give me what I want."

"What do you want?" Ava asked skeptically, crossing her arms over her chest.

"To find my maker."

"Any witch worth her salt could have used his name to find him," Ava argued.

"I don't know his name. Or who he is," Macgrath explained. "I woke on this earth with no memory of my past and I want to know why."

I could feel the truth of his words. His heart was pure, even if his mind was a seething mass of confusion.

"I still think we should imprison him or turn him into the vampire council," Ava muttered, her expression dark.

"The vampire council will know what to do with him and where his maker is," I agreed.

"No!" Savannah argued, moving to stand in front of Macgrath. "Look, do this for me, please. Let him go tonight. If he causes any more trouble, then you can turn him into the council."

I didn't want to agree, but I could sense her resolve. She wouldn't give this up. Ava and I exchanged a glance of mutual frustration. Ava's jaw clenched and she nodded slightly. Even she understood that Savannah had dug in her heels and there would be no changing her mind.

"Fine," Ava relented. She moved closer, pointing a finger at Macgrath. "But I will be watching you. If you put so much as a toe out of line, I will make you wish you'd never come to Austin."

"I already wish that," he retorted. "But I won't be staying here."

Ava glared at him. The closer she stood to him, the brighter the chain between them glowed. I wondered why neither of them seemed to notice it.

Savannah smiled happily at Ava before she turned toward Macgrath. "Thank you for protecting me. I hope you find what you're looking for."

The vampire's face softened in a way I didn't like. "Thank you, Savannah."

With that, he backed away and melted into the darkness.

After he was gone, Savannah came over to me and wrapped her arms around my waist.

"I'm ready to go home," she murmured into my chest.

CHAPTER TWENTY-SEVEN

Savannah

ON THE WAY back to Austin, I'd looked at Rhys and said, "I'm starving. Want to grab a burger?" Both he and Ava had stared at me in shocked silence for a few seconds. Still, as soon as we reached the city, Rhys steered the SUV into the parking lot of a burger chain and pulled into the drive thru.

I hadn't spoken at all as I sat on the floor of my living room and devoured my food. Now my burger was gone and the events of the night were crashing down on me. The trash from our late night burger run littered my coffee table and I munched on leftover fries as I told Ava and Rhys about my day with Macgrath.

"He never hurt me. Even when I was kicking him or trying to punch him, he was gentle. He didn't even leave a bruise on me."

"That doesn't matter," Ava fumed. "He *kidnapped* you right out of my fucking store!"

"Language!" I chided her. "You know I don't like it when you curse so much." I neglected to mention exactly how much I swore when I was fighting Macgrath. It was better if she didn't know about that.

Ava just glared at me. "I still don't like it. We should have called the council in Dallas."

I looked at Rhys, who was reclined on the couch. "What do

you think, Rhys? Do you think it was a mistake to let him go?"

He sighed and rubbed his hands over his face. "Yes," he muttered. "Savannah, he took you from me. He threatened you. For that alone, I want to suck the life from him and burn his carcass."

My nose crinkled at his statement. "Eww."

Ava snorted. "Yeah, the visual there is kinda gross, Rhys."

He shrugged. "It's the truth." His eyes came to me. "But it's also the truth that his heart is good. He allowed his desperation for answers to blind him to her true nature."

I smiled at him. "He's more like you than you realize."

Rhys shook his head. "I don't think so."

I didn't respond, merely took a sip of my drink. He was wrong. Rhys had been searching for a home when he moved in across the street. Macgrath wanted the same thing, even if he didn't understand that yet. He claimed he wanted to find his maker, but I knew it was more. He yearned for the sort of relationship a maker often had with their vampire children. He yearned for home.

Satchel pranced into the living room, straight to me, meowing all the way. She sat down in front of me and grumbled for several seconds.

"Is she talking to you again? What's she saying?" Ava asked.

I reached out and stroked Satchel's back. "She's just letting me know that she didn't appreciate being left alone for so long today." The cat purred as she walked forward and butted her head against my waist. "And that she's glad I'm home."

Ava shook her head. "You two are so weird." She drank down the rest of her wine. "And I still think it was stupid to let that damn vampire go."

I rolled my eyes. "Speaking of letting things go, why don't you free that thought? You're driving me nuts."

"Savannah," Ava began.

"No, I don't want to hear it," I stated, lifting a hand. "You and

Rhys have made your feelings on the matter clear enough. You aren't going to change my mind and I'm not going to change yours."

"Fine," Ava relented. "What happened after you tried to climb out of the bathroom window?"

"Well, he made mushroom risotto and roasted asparagus for dinner. I didn't eat much but it was good."

Ava groaned and let her head fall back on the couch. "Okay, maybe not that much information. I don't care if he can cook."

"Okay, how about this? Rhiannon helped Gaius make Cornelius and Rhys, but with an ulterior motive in mind. She never said what that was, but I'm pretty sure I've figured it out."

"To increase her power," Rhys stated.

I nodded, sipping my drink again as I petted Satchel. "I think so."

"The legends," Ava murmured.

"I don't think they're legends, Ava," I replied. "I think that Rhiannon wanted Gaius to create the *animavore* with that intent in mind. Their purpose was to increase her power. What she didn't count on was how strong they would be in their own right. I think Cornelius was too strong for her and that he was going to turn the tables on her. She had to run for her life. Just like she did tonight."

Rhys cocked his head to the side. "I've always been weaker than Cornelius. Why didn't she come after me?"

I shook my head. "I don't think she knew about you until Cornelius was dead. I think that's why Gaius made you after he turned Cornelius. He didn't want her to know that he had two test subjects. That would certainly explain how you escaped her notice for so long."

Rhys didn't look convinced, but I couldn't think of another explanation. "She's still out there," he commented.

Ava nodded. "Yes, but what Savannah did...it depleted Rhiannon's power. She's not as strong as she was before. It will take time for her to rebuild her strength."

"And she doesn't have Macgrath to help her any longer," I pointed out.

Ava rolled her eyes. "She might. For all you know, he went straight to her when he left us in the field tonight."

I shook my head. "I don't think so. He's done with her. We'll be okay."

"We'll see," Rhys replied. He rose from the floor. "I'm going to take a shower and get ready for bed."

I was grateful that he was giving me time alone with Ava. There were things I wanted to discuss with her.

He leaned over and gave me a kiss before disappearing down the hall to my bedroom. Satchel jumped off my lap and darted out of the living room after him.

Unconcerned with my pet's abandonment, I turned toward Ava.

"What?" she asked defensively.

"When were you going to tell me?"

"Tell you what?" She wouldn't meet my gaze.

"That you've been touched by the Goddess." I'd known as soon as I saw her floating there above Rhiannon's protection circle that she was more than a witch. Her hair was longer and brighter and her eyes had changed to an intense purple. I could see the glow of the goddess emanating from within her, a light that hurt to look at even though it was no brighter than a candle.

Being touched by the god or goddess meant they shared a piece of their power with you, that they acknowledged you as their child. Being touched by the deities should offer you protection. Witches and warlocks, both light and dark, acknowledged the deities. Most wouldn't risk incurring the wrath of the god or goddess and avoided those who had been touched.

Ava rubbed her hand over her forehead. "I don't remember much about it. Just that the goddess gave me power when I needed it. I can't even remember why. Then one night I woke up on the ground next to a stream. I couldn't remember how I got there or where I had been before. Small parts of my past have come back to me over the centuries, but there is so much that is still a blur."

"Why didn't you tell me any of this before?" I asked, feeling hurt. Ava and I had been friends for a decade.

"It's not something I like to talk about," she murmured. Her gaze finally met mine and her indigo and violet eyes were sad. "You've always said that you were lost when you met me, that I made your life better." Her smile didn't reach her eyes. "But you should consider that it was you who made my life better. There are things…" she trailed off and then swallowed hard. "Things I don't talk about because they hurt. Just thinking about them, like right now, hurts too badly. Even after centuries."

I could sense the pain welling inside her. They were emotions she usually kept tightly leashed. I pushed myself off the floor and went to sit next to her on the sofa. She hugged me close and her breathing was ragged. A few moments later, she released me and leaned back. Her eyes were bright but dry as though she had fought back tears and won.

"I love you, Savannah Baker," she stated. "You are the sister I always wanted."

"I love you too, Ava."

She kissed my cheek. "Now, I'm going to go home and get some sleep. Then tomorrow I'm going to get up and order a new mattress for Rhys' house because that thing is uncomfortable as hell."

"I don't think it'll matter much longer," I replied.

She grinned. "Why do you say that?"

"I'm going to ask him to move in with me."

"You're going to live in sin? What would your grandmother say?" she teased.

"Probably *'Good for you. He's a hot piece of ass.'* "

Ava burst out laughing. "No way. I don't think I ever heard your grandmother cuss."

I shrugged. "The only time in my life I heard her say that word was when she was talking about Cary Grant."

Ava frowned slightly. "Cary Grant?"

"Grandma had refined tastes."

We both giggled for a minute as we remembered my grandmother and her feistiness.

"Thank you for coming for me tonight," I said quietly.

Ava took my hand. "I'll always come for you, babe." She got up from the sofa. "Now, walk me to the door then go into your bedroom and make out with your man. Oh, and the store is closed for the next couple of days. Then I'm going to hire a manager. It's time."

I did as she asked, walking her to the door. After one last hug, I watched her climb into her car and drive away. I closed the door, taking the time to lock it, and walked through the house checking the lights and windows. Though I doubted that Macgrath or Rhiannon would be back tonight, I wasn't going to take any chances.

When I got to the bedroom, Rhys was pulling on a pair of loose cotton shorts. "Hey, how are you feeling?" he asked.

"Tired, but I need to shower. I'll be right back."

I took the shortest shower possible and did nothing more than towel dry my hair. I nearly wept when I came out of the stall and found one of the baggy t-shirts I liked to sleep in and a pair of panties lying on the counter, neatly folded. I slipped into them and walked into the bedroom. Rhys was already in bed, leaning back against the pillows with his arms behind his head.

He looked over at me when I came out of the bathroom and asked, "Feeling better?"

I nodded and walked around the bed, climbing beneath the covers when he threw them back for me. I scooted over until my cheek rested on his shoulder and his arm wrapped around me. "Thank you."

"For what?" he asked.

"Everything," I answered. "You've given me everything I've ever wanted."

CHAPTER TWENTY-EIGHT

Rhys

THE NEXT MORNING, I woke up before Savannah. In reality, I'd barely slept at all. As the sun came up and light began to creep around the curtains in her bedroom, I looked down at my woman. She looked peaceful and relaxed in my arms, as though the frightening events of the previous day didn't touch her mind.

I watched her beloved face in the changing light and knew that I would never hesitate to do whatever was necessary to protect her. She had become the center of my world.

The fear that I felt yesterday would take a long time to forget. As would the sight of Savannah trapped behind the red glow of Rhiannon's circle, staring at me in sheer terror.

Suddenly, I was seized by the need to show Savannah how much she meant to me, to make sure she knew that I couldn't live without her. I needed to touch her and reassure myself that she was safe and whole.

Her back was pressed to my front, her knees bent. My body curved into the shape of hers, clinging together from shoulders to thigh. I slid my hand beneath the hem of her shirt, lifting the fabric as I trailed my fingertips over her skin. She was warm and soft with sleep, her breathing deep and even.

When my hand moved over the mound of her breast, she

sighed in her sleep and arched her back. Burying my face against her neck, I kissed her skin, running my tongue over her throat. She moaned softly and shifted against me, pressing her hips into mine and rubbing her ass over my shaft.

I cupped her breast, massaging her nipple with my palm. Savannah moaned again, her body undulating against me. My cock grew hard as she moved.

"Rhys?" Her sleepy voice was lower and rougher than usual.

When she tried to turn around, I stopped her. "No, just let me touch you."

She whimpered as my fingers tugged at her nipples before running down the center of her stomach. I moved my knee between hers and hooked her leg over my thigh, lifting it. Savannah gasped as my fingers delved into her underwear, seeking her center. She was hot and wet, her head tilting back as her hips moved against my hand.

"Oh, God, Rhys," she whimpered, rocking into my touch.

I slid my fingers through the wetness between her thighs and circled her clit lightly. As her movements became more frantic and her breath began to quicken, I increased the pressure of my fingers. I locked my mouth on her shoulder, biting lightly as she cried out, coming apart beneath my touch.

As the spasms rocked her body, I turned her onto her back and rolled on top of her. I reached into the nightstand and grabbed a condom, quickly jerking down my shorts, dealing with the wrapper, and rolling it over myself. During the last few weeks, I'd learned how to put the shield on and take it off without a mess.

Once the condom was taken care of, I guided myself inside her body, thrusting slow and deep. Savannah arched her back, her hands grasping my back until her nails bit into my skin. Her dark eyes stared up at me, still a little sleepy and hazy from her climax. I leaned down and kissed her, moving deeper and harder with each stroke.

She didn't hesitate to meet my mouth, making a soft noise as our lips clung together.

I shoved one arm beneath her hips and cupped the back of her skull with my other hand, lifting her into my thrusts. Her body tightened around me and her head fell back as she cried out. I knew she was getting close to the peak once again. I pushed her harder, moving faster, until her body locked around me and her hand fisted in my hair.

"Rhys!"

I rode out the waves of her orgasm until I came hard. I slammed inside her one last time and buried my face in her neck. As our bodies settled, Savannah's hands ran over my back, her fingers dragging over my skin.

When I lifted my head, she smiled up at me. "Good morning."

I smiled in return. "Good morning, Savannah."

"It certainly is," she murmured.

I laughed softly as I pulled out of her, rolling out of bed so I could dispose of the condom in the bathroom.

When I returned, she was curled up on her side, her hands folded beneath her cheek. I climbed beneath the blankets and lay facing her. "What should we do today?" I asked her. For the last few weeks, we'd barely left the house except to go to *The Magic Bean*. "Please tell me Ava isn't opening the shop."

Savannah smiled and shook her head. "No, she said she's taking the next couple of days off." Her grin widened. "And she said that she's hiring a manager so she can have more time to herself."

I wouldn't believe that until I saw it. "So we have the whole day together."

She nodded then bit her lip. "I did have an idea of what we could do today."

"What's that?"

"Well, you've practically been living here for the past few weeks anyway, so I thought we could move the rest of your stuff into the house," she replied. "Make it official."

"Official? Wouldn't that be marriage?"

Savannah went utterly still, her dark eyes boring into mine. "Maybe, though I think less than six months together might be a little early to start talking about marriage."

"So we can discuss it again in four months?"

She laughed. "If you still want to, yes, we can."

"I've told you once before, Savannah. I will always be here. As long as you love me, as long as you want me, I'll be here. And probably even if you don't."

Her eyes danced. "I should probably find that last statement creepy, but I don't. I like hearing it." Her smile faded as she looked at me. Cupping my cheek in her hand, she said, "I love you, Rhys. I'm so glad that your destiny brought you to my door."

"I love you too, though I think you were the one who came to my door first."

"That's true," she said with a smile. "Though you were so good-looking I had no idea half of what I was saying."

"Hm, tell me more," I invited her, inching closer.

Savannah shook her head. "No way." She turned her head and glanced at the clock. "We should probably get up. I'm sure it'll take most of the day to pack your stuff and get it over here."

"Not really. I only had one bag of clothes and a box of books when I moved in."

Her eyes widened. "That's all."

Wrapping an arm around her, I rolled over onto my back and pulled her on top of my chest. "It'll take us an hour at most."

She hummed in her throat. "Then what will we do for the rest of the day."

Grinning, I pulled her down for a kiss. "I'm sure we'll think of something," I murmured against her mouth.

SEVERAL HOURS LATER, I left a note for Savannah, who was sleeping in the bed, and walked across the street to the rental house. As soon as I entered, my cell phone rang. I removed it from my pocket and smiled when I saw the name on the screen.

"Kerry," I greeted her.

"From the tone of your voice, I'm assuming things worked out for you and your new lady. You know, since you *didn't call me* and let me know."

"I'm sorry," I apologized.

"I'll let it slide since I knew anyway, but next time I expect a phone call."

"Of course."

"And I also expect an invitation to the wedding," she stated.

I laughed. "There won't be a wedding. At least not anytime soon."

"Rhys, don't tell me that you aren't willing to marry that sweet woman," she warned.

"Oh, I'm willing and ready. She's the one who doesn't want get married so soon."

Kerry laughed loud and long. "I really need to meet her. What's her name?"

"Savannah Baker."

Kerry was silent for a long moment. "Savannah Baker? Was her grandmother Tawna Baker?"

"I don't know."

"Shit, it would figure that you would move to Austin and find the granddaughter of the greatest seer the last century has ever seen. She was an amazing woman."

I stopped what I was doing and stared across the street. "She was a seer?"

"Yes, one of the most powerful I've ever heard of."

"But Savannah is an empath."

Kerry paused. "It happens sometimes. Different talents emerge in the bloodline. Is that a problem?"

"No, it's not. Just a surprise."

"So, when do I get to meet her?" Kerry asked.

"When can you come to Austin?"

"Sooner than you think."

"I can't wait to introduce you two to Ava, Savannah's boss and my landlord. I think you'll like her."

"Then I'm sure I will." She paused. "We need to talk."

I blew out a breath. "I know."

"No, you don't know, Rhys," she shot back. "The day you called me, I found something my mother left for me. A vision spell." Kerry hesitated for a brief moment. "And Rhiannon was in it."

"Explain," I demanded, my throat tight with anger and sudden fear.

"She's old. Older even than you. And powerful. The things that she's done..." Kerry trailed off. "She's not going to stop until she gets what she wants."

"What does she want?" I asked. "Do you know?"

"She wants to become the goddess, Rhys. She wants to dethrone the deity and take her place. That is her only goal."

A cold chill drifted through me. Ava and Savannah had discussed this last night, but it was only speculation. Kerry spoke of it as though it were fact.

"I won't let that happen." I could feel the sparks from my fingers snapping at the phone I held pressed to my ear. Even with Kerry's amulet, my power was surging due to my rage. I took a deep breath, searching for calm.

"Rhys, she's still out there and you have no idea where. You'll need our help."

"Fine. Come visit, search for Rhiannon, meet my woman, and I'll introduce you to Ava."

"Wonderful. We'll see you soon."

She disconnected and I put my phone back in my pocket. I realized that in the last year, I'd made friends and learned how to live my life again. For centuries, I had walked on this earth living less than half a life.

Meeting Savannah, I found everything I didn't realize I wanted. She gave me love and she gave me a home. I hadn't realized it until this morning when she said I gave her everything, but she had done the same for me.

Savannah was everything to me and I would be damned if I would let a power hungry witch do anything to tear us apart.

EPILOGUE

Ava

I STUDIED THE young man sitting across the table from me. He looked vaguely familiar, but I couldn't place him. Still, he was the only applicant for the manager position, so I couldn't afford to be choosy.

"Harrison, it says here that you're a graduate student at UT. What are you studying?"

"Art history," he replied.

"Do you have any teaching assistantships that will require your time?"

"Not this summer or next semester. After that, I'm not sure."

I appreciated his honesty, though the way his eyes kept dropping to my breasts might become a problem. I didn't want to fend off the advances of a horny college student, but I was desperate. I needed someone to keep things running at the store. I would have preferred a witch, but most of the witches I knew considered themselves above making coffee. They would help customers with the books, amulets, and candles, but they would flat out refuse to make a latte.

"I have a question, if you don't mind," Harrison said, interrupting my train of thought.

"Of course," I replied with a smile.

"I see you have a reading room here, what services do you offer?"

My brows lifted in surprise. "Tarot, palmistry, and tea leaves."

He nodded. "No futures?"

I squinted at him. "No. I don't currently employ a seer."

"What about the spell books, candles, and amulets? Do you actually prepare the spells for the customers or do they mostly come in for supplies?"

"Most of the customers prefer to make their own potions and charms, so they buy supplies separately. From time to time, I'll make them if the customer is having difficulty or doesn't have the talent necessary. Will that be a problem?"

Harrison shook his head. "No, not at all. It sounds as if you're running a very responsible business that deals in magic."

I bit back a smile. "How old are you, Harrison?" I asked him.

"I'll be forty on my next birthday."

My eyes widened. "Forty?"

He grinned, revealing sharp canines. "I'm a shifter. We tend to look young until we reach our fifties or sixties."

My witch's sense quivered. I hadn't recognized him for a shifter and he hadn't set off any alarms within the store. "I'm surprised I didn't recognize you for what you are," I commented calmly as my brain whirled, thinking of ways to defend myself.

The shifter lifted a hand. "There is no reason to fear me, Ava," he stated. "I'm here about the job, but I wanted you to give me a fair chance."

"So you disarmed my wards and spells and misled me?" I asked. Shifters shouldn't even have the capability, which meant he had magic in his bloodlines as well. What really ticked me off is that the sneaky bastard had gotten away with it until now. I couldn't afford to have weaknesses in my security. Not with Rhiannon on the loose.

He sighed. "I wanted to be certain you were using your abilities ethically before I told you what I was."

"I'm not sure I'll be able to trust you after this," I stated, studying him closely.

"I can understand if that's the case." He got to his feet. "If I don't hear from you, I'll take it as a statement that you've decided to hire someone else." The tone of his voice suggested he wouldn't care one way or another, which made me like him a little. Damn the hairy pup.

I watched him leave and waited until the door shut behind him. Lifting a hand, I twisted the lock with a quick spell. Something about him unsettled me and it wasn't just the way he ogled my breasts. But I also liked the idea of having someone who was knowledgeable around so that I wouldn't have to be. The fact that he understood magic and he was willing to make coffee and serve pastry made him the perfect candidate. Which put me in a difficult position.

I decided to worry about it tomorrow. After a good night's sleep, I would have a better grasp of the situation. I hoped.

I got up and turned out the lights. I'd kept the shop open later than usual so I could meet Harrison for his interview. Now it was getting late and I was ready to go home, drink a glass of wine, and take a bubble bath before bed.

"Just another night in my glamorous life," I murmured to myself as I walked through the storeroom to my office.

"Very glamorous indeed." At the low male voice, I whirled, lifting my hands to defend myself. When I saw who it was, I very nearly zapped him with a good bolt of electricity anyway, just to teach him a lesson.

"What are you doing here?" I asked, lowering my arms. "And how did you get in?"

The vampire was leaning against the wall, his arms crossed over his chest as he watched me. "That little pup disarmed all your wards, even the ones in the back. I decided to wait inside in case you needed my help."

I scoffed. "Macgrath, the day I need your help is the day hell freezes over."

"No man is an island, Ava," he stated. "Or woman in this case."

I rolled my eyes and gathered my things from my desk. "What does that even mean?" I asked him sarcastically.

"That you can't do everything alone. No one makes it through life without help from someone, sometime."

I bit back a sigh. My question had mostly been rhetorical because I did understand the expression well enough. "That's true," I agreed. "But there's nothing in my life that obligates me to taking your help."

"I'm offering it freely, whether you take it or not."

He straightened and stalked towards me. Though I wanted to back away, I held my ground. He didn't intimidate me but he made me feel things that I didn't want to feel. In close quarters, I couldn't ignore the way my skin heated or my heart raced.

I would never admit to anyone, much less myself, but Macgrath was sexy as hell. He made my body hum with desire and the bastard knew it.

"If you're that cheap, I definitely don't want anything you offer me," I retorted.

"Why do you fight me on everything?" he asked, his eyes moving over my face.

"Because you kidnapped my best friend!" I cried. "Oh and let's not forget the years you spent with a psychobitch witch." I hesitated. Shit, I hadn't meant to rhyme.

The corners of his mouth twitched. "I've made mistakes."

I shook my head, feeling my ire rise. "Mistakes? You call everything you've done mistakes?"

"You don't understand what it feels like to not know who you are," he stated gruffly. "To want someone, *anyone*, to know you and care about you."

I glared up at him. "I do know what that feels like," I snapped. "But you don't see me going around kidnapping people or helping crazy witches." I realized we were standing mere inches apart and jerked back. "Why are you here?" I asked angrily.

He followed me each time I tried to put space between us until my back bumped the wall. Macgrath leaned over me, placing his palm on the wall above my head, looming over me. "Because I can't stay away from you," he answered. He looked as angry about it as I felt. "There is something between us, Ava, a connection. I know you feel it even though you pretend not to."

"I don't," I denied. "And what you're doing is called stalking."

"You don't feel anything for me?"

"I wouldn't say that," I shot back. "Though most of the words used to describe my feelings shouldn't be used in mixed company."

"That's not why your heart beats faster. Or why your scent changes. You want me, even though you hate it."

His body drew closer and I could feel that connection he mentioned as it flared between us. I wanted to touch him and have him touch me, but I resisted.

"I don't,' I denied again.

"I'll prove it," he said and somehow it sounded like a threat.

Before I could tell him to back off, his head lowered and he kissed me. His mouth was rough and demanding. And delicious.

I made a noise in the back of my throat as I let Macgrath take my weight. Immediately, his arms circled me, dragging me closer to his hard body. When his tongue slid between my lips, I stopped trying to resist and clutched at his waist. His torso was hot and unforgiving as he pressed my back against the wall.

When his palms skimmed over my shoulders and down to my breasts, I moaned, arching against him. My tongue danced with his until it brushed his sharp fang. The slight sting brought me back to my senses and I twisted my head away.

"Stop," I panted. "Macgrath."

When I said his name, he rested his forehead against my shoulder as he struggled to control himself. After a few long moments, he stepped back and slowly removed his hands from my body.

I pressed my palms against the wall, using it to hold myself up when my legs were too weak.

Macgrath and I stared at each other in silence. My chest moved quickly as I struggled to slow my breathing and I could see the brilliant gleam of his eyes in the shadows of the storeroom.

"I'll see you soon," he whispered as he disappeared in the darkness, the glow of his eyes fading away.

I shivered at the rough sound of his voice.

Because I knew that his words were a promise.

The End

***The Blood & Bone series will continue with
Ava and Macgrath's story in Fall 2017.***

Sign Up for C.C.'s Monthly Newsletter

www.ccwood.net/newsletter

Blogger Sign Up for C.C.'s Master List:

http://bit.ly/2mieXgm

<u>Contact C.C.</u>

C.C. loves to hear from her readers!

Facebook:

www.facebook.com/authorccwood

CC's Sinners (Reader Group):

http://bit.ly/CCSinners

Twitter:

www.twitter.com/cc_wood

Instagram:

www.instagram.com/authorccwood

Pinterest:

www.pinterest.com/ccwood01

Email:

author@ccwood.net

You can also sign up for blog updates and C.C.'s monthly newsletter on her website!

www.ccwood.net

About C.C.

Born and raised in Texas, C.C. Wood writes saucy paranormal and contemporary romances featuring strong, sassy women and the men that love them. If you ever meet C.C. in person, keep in mind that many of her characters are based on people she knows, so anything you say or do is likely to end up in a book one day.

A self-professed hermit, C.C. loves to stay home, where she reads, writes, cooks, and watches TV. She can usually be found drinking coffee or wine as she spends time with her hubby, daughter, and two beagles.

Titles by C.C. Wood

Novellas:

Girl Next Door Series:

Friends with Benefits

Frenemies

Drive Me Crazy

Girl Next Door — The Complete Series

Kiss Series:

A Kiss for Christmas

Kiss Me

Novels:

Seasons of Sorrow

NSFW Series:

In Love With Lucy

Earning Yancy

Tempting Tanya

Westfall Brothers Series:

Texas with a Twist

Wicked Games Series:

All or Nothing

Paranormal Romance:

Bitten Series:
Bite Me
Once Bitten, Twice Shy
Bewitched, Bothered, and Bitten
One Little Bite
Love Bites
Bite the Bullet

Blood & Bone Series (Bitten spin-off)
Blood & Bone
Souls Unchained
Destined by Blood

Cozy Paranormal:

The Wraith Files:
Don't Wake the Dead
The Dead Come Calling

Made in the USA
Middletown, DE
04 June 2021